NATIVE SPIRIT

Native Spirit

The Story of Saint Kateri Tekakwitha

ANNE CASTELL

NATIVE SPIRIT, Copyright © 2014 by Anne Castell. All rights reserved. Printed in the United States of America. For information, address PO Box 799, Menifee, CA 92586

Cover design by Anne Castell.

ISBN-13: 978-1500486624
ISBN-10: 1500486620

First Edition: July 2014

To my husband for all his patience

CHAPTER ONE

Iroquioa 1672

She looked upward, listening to the wind fleeing through the drying cornstalks. The sky was not blue today, but gray like the underbelly of a trout. Its brightness still made her squint. Most light did, no matter how dim.

A dark shape circled above. Blurry, the shape could be a hawk as easily as a buzzard, though with patience and careful watching, she slowly came to realize it was, indeed, a hawk. Perhaps there were rabbits in the cornfield. Or mice. "Your eyesight is still good," she said aloud to the bird. "And a good thing. You would starve if *you* could not see."

Saying the words only reminded her of her conversation with her uncle, the chief, only yesterday. "Tekakwitha," he had said, an angry sound coming from his blurred features. "You must agree on a husband, or you will surely starve. You are sixteen summers now. Who will care for you when I am too old?"

"What husband would want a blind wife?" she had replied, fingers busy with her stitches.

He reached down and grabbed the buckskin from her hands. He examined the embroidery with tiny shells, porcupine quills, and

1

white man's beads. "For a blind wife, you sew well. Better than some with all their sight."

Tekakwitha lowered her filmy eyes. "The women of my father's village have always been kind to me. They taught me. I can do small things, close things. Here in Gandawague, I have become used to where things are without stumbling." She lowered her face and felt her cheeks heat with blushing. "But what of greater things? There is much I cannot do."

He shook his head. "There is little you do *not* do." He chuckled, his sternness seemingly forgotten. "You think of distant worries and not of nearer ones. Think of a husband."

Yet today, under the glossy sky and the watchful gaze of the hawk, Tekakwitha thought not of husbands, but of distant birdsong, trilling in echoes across the nearby meadow; of the soft step of the does and her fawn just at the edge of the dark green wood behind her; of the wide sky and the big salty waters just over the hills. "Shonkwaia'tishon," she said to the Creator of All, "I have never asked you why the white man's pox hurt my face and my eyes." She could not help raising her fingers to the familiar ugly scars marring her features. "Nor have I asked why this sickness took the lives of my mother, my father, and my baby brother so long ago, for you are wise and know ways I do not. But I ask that you tell me, Shonkwaia'tishon—if you will—what decision should I make? My uncle says I need a husband like all maidens do. It is every girl's wish to have a place of her own in the longhouse, her own man, her own children, making the flat corn cakes over her own fire. Why is this such an empty wish to me? Why is the song of the wind more powerful in my mind than the voice of warriors?"

The dry stalks rustled and she reached up, delicately touching a yellowed leaf. The harvest was already taken, and Uncle told her to go to the cornfield to thank the corn gods for the bounty.

She watched the sway of stalks against the flat sky. They brushed past one another, pressing close, grasping one another's leaves in woven patterns. She knew she was supposed to thank the corn gods, but thinking of them left such an unexplainable emptiness inside, that her lips stayed tightly shut.

Again she raised her head, and the stalks wove in the wind, finally forming a cross and holding that shape for a long moment. She blinked and watched the cross shudder under the wind's breath, until the stalks suddenly released, opening her sight again to the bright autumn sky.

It was like her dream. Dreams often came to her, sometimes at night, but sometimes also during the day. She could have talked of these dreams at the Midwinter festival. This was the time for dream-telling, but these dreams happened all the time now, and she wondered if she should tell it to someone. She saw the cross often, too, but perhaps it reminded her of her mother who wore such a shape around her neck.

Tekakwitha remembered touching that cross with younger fingers those many years ago, when she was only four years old. She also recalled how her mother took it carefully out of her hand, glancing anxiously toward the door of the longhouse. "It is not safe to be a Christian among the Mohawks," her Algonquin mother had said. She used to tell Tekakwitha how her people fought, and how she was captured by the Mohawks, and that the women of her village of Osseneron decided she would be a slave.

"What is Christian?" Tekakwitha had asked, but the sad-faced woman with the long black hair only shook her head.

"It is the God I believe in," she whispered. "Even though your father he chief took me out of slavery and made me a member of the Turtle Clan, he told me I am not to worship this God here."

"Why not?"

"Hush, child. You ask so many questions." And so she was rocked gently to sleep in her mother's arms, almost the last time for such peacefulness. It was not long after that day that a warrior staggered into the village, covered in the terrible rash that meant the white man's smallpox. No one was spared. All seemed to fall ill, including Tekakwitha and her family. When her family died, her uncle, the chief's brother, moved into her father's longhouse and took the sickly Tekakwitha in.

Did the dreams begin then, she wondered?

Tekakwitha rose, brushing the soil from her buckskin skirt and pulling strands of old corn silk from her dark braids. Distracted, she left the field, neglecting to thank the corn gods.

It was the time of day to grind the corn into meal, and Tekakwitha was anxious to join the other women at the grinding stones. She knew the way, though it appeared like a shadowy path to her injured eyes. Confident, her moccasin steps moved swiftly over the stones.

She heard their laughter first until she saw the indistinct tawny figures bent over the grinding, and took her place easily beside them. There was no stumbling to reach the women like there was in the past when she was younger. She was older now, and even at sixteen earned her place of respect among the women. Even her name—Tekakwitha, which means "she who stumbles"—could no longer be used against her as it was when she was a child, truly stumbling her way through a village she could barely see.

"Did you get lost?" asked Wild Flower, glancing her way.

Wild Flower's high-pitched voice and round face was so distinctive, that Tekakwitha could pick her out in the distance.

"I was in the cornfield," she said, offering no more than that.

Wild Flower shrugged and turned from her, chatting brightly to the others, knowing Tekakwitha would not join in their conversation of gossip and jokes.

Tekakwitha thought of little while she pushed the stone over the corn to grind it over the rough, flat rock. Through the vibration in her hands, she could feel the hard kernels split and crack, crumbling into meal. The rhythm of the stone on stone soothed her into daydreaming. She imagined she was running with the deer into the dark thickets.

"Tekakwitha!"

She awoke to the sound of her name and looked up, squinting at the blurry faces. They laughed, mocking her daydreaming. *It was not idleness*, she longed to say aloud. It was more like being taken a long distance and shown something just out of reach. It was only the tip of something greater, like the blue-tinted chunks of ice floating in the Mohawk River. Atop, the ice looked small, but below the rushing river waters, they were large and mysterious. This thing that kept touching her mind held no danger, but it lay deeply hidden, like acorns buried by squirrels. If she could only move the dead leaves of her muddled thoughts, she might be able to see, to understand...

"Tekakwitha! Have you gone deaf now, too?"

"Forgive me," she said. "You were saying?"

"We were talking of husbands, or would-be husbands," said Wild Flower. She nudged Tekakwitha in the shoulder and giggled, causing Tekakwitha's cheeks to burn. "Your uncle, the chief, must be choosing the best warrior for you."

Slowly, Tekakwitha began grinding the grain again. "I do not know."

"You do not know?" laughed Wild Flower to the others, who joined in the laughter. "Of course you should know! You will have to make the final choice. Who is it, Tekakwitha? Is it the one who stands beside your uncle at the festivals?"

"He has skinny legs," commented the pregnant woman. She stretched her back and rubbed her swollen belly.

"But the rest of him looks strong enough," said Wild Flower. Her round face turned again toward Tekakwitha. "Which is it?"

"No one," she said quietly, trying to return to grinding the corn, until Wild Flower's hand reached out to grasp her wrist.

"No one? It must be someone special if she will not say."

Tekakwitha said nothing. Let them believe what they will. It was every maiden's desire to have a husband, yet it was not hers. The wind again called Tekakwitha, and she turned her mind inward, thinking of hidden things, the things of Shonkwaia'tishon, trying to understand his distant meanings, seeing her mother's face in the midst of it...and always the shape of the cross.

Fall was a busy time. All of Gandawague prepared or the winter hunt not too far away. Tekakwitha busied herself gathering the last sap from maple trees to make the sweet syrup before the sap was gone for the winter. The strong scent of burnt sugar from the syrup tents lifted into the air, reminding her that time was short. Sap would have to be collected before the snows so that it could be cooked in the big iron kettles and rendered down to sweet golden syrup. *Bees and honey, and trees and syrup,* she thought merrily. That such sweetness could be coaxed from the Creator's wilderness! He was a great provider indeed. She thanked him before rushing busily from tree to tree with her buckets, slashing another gash into the bark. She brought her face close to the slender trunk to see if the sap ran freely. She liked this time and this season. So many of the villagers were busy at their own tasks that they did not bother her. "It is not that I do not love my people," she said to the icy wind blowing up from the creek. "But I am glad to be alone sometimes, and think about the many spirits in the land and how grateful I am for such bounty."

It was good to listen to the fluted call of the loon off the Mohawk River and feel the dead leaves crackle under her moccasins. The trees, too, burst into the colors of flames, crimsons and oranges and fiery yellows. Shonkwaia'tishon was not preparing for the poverty of winter, but the riches of great chiefs, cloaking himself in this fire.

"Great Shonkwaia'tishon," she murmured, affixing the bucket to the tree to catch the precious sap. "I can almost see you cloaked in such glorious flames, and it fills me with such love and longing for you." She stopped and raised her face to the icy weather, squinting into the tangle of black twigs against a dark gray sky. The thought filled her mind with questions. "Where does such longing come from?" she asked the wind, astonished that such swelling emotions for the distant Creator should engulf her. "I know it is our duty to thank you for all you have created, but why this longing? Uncle would say I should rather long for a husband, but it is not so. Is that so misguided?"

The idea of the fiery cloak of Shonkwaia'tishon made her smile, until the sudden image of a cross against that cloak turned down the edges of her mouth. "Great Creator, why do I see this shape, this cross? What meaning has it for me?"

A twig snapped and the echo of hoof falls brought her head jerking upward. She listened, tilting her head. The others were back in the village. It could not be them. Carefully, she crouched and moved forward between the tall straight stands of maple trees. Movement ahead alerted her to the intruders, but her damaged eyes could tell her nothing. She moved closer, ducking behind a thicket of winding blackberry vines. After a cautious breath, she raised her head.

Three horses tramped heavily over the forest path, their metal bridles jangling like small festival bells. Their breath unfurled about their long muzzles in foggy clouds while they carried their dark charge forward. Tekakwitha squinted, and then her eyes widened in fear.

One man road atop a horse, trailing two packhorses behind. He was not Mohawk. Not even a French trapper that the chief disliked but tolerated. This man was different. She knew something of him, the kind of man he was. But his sudden appearance in the village meant that bad things might happen, strange things.

"Blackrobe," she whispered.

CHAPTER TWO

Tekakwitha's uncle scowled at the Blackrobe. She knew from talk of the others that this solitary man was a Jesuit priest, but was called a Blackrobe by the Iroquois because of the long gown he and others like him wore. She knew he was Christian like her mother, and she also saw the wooden cross laying on his chest, symbol of his faith. Standing behind her aunt, she listened to the Blackrobe trying to make himself understood through he did not speak the People's language.

Tekakwitha remember the tales told around the campfires when the first Blackrobes came many years ago, and how the Mohawks killed them. But more and more followed, and more white men besides, so it was finally agreed in the Iroquois Confederacy of the five Indian nations to stop the fighting between themselves and the French white men, even allowing them to trap and trade in their territory. Always, the white men would break treaty after treaty, but the Iroquois soon realized that fighting would not stop the white men from flowing into their lands like a river flooding its banks. The Blackrobes came, too, bringing trouble and new ideas to the villages.

Tekakwitha's uncle listened to the white priest, who was trying to explain what he wanted. His scowl deepened the more the priest was understood. At last the chief turned to his wife who stood with the other women elders of the village. "He wishes to build a...a 'chapel' here. He wishes to bring their god to us."

"Why?" asked her aunt. She cast a wary glance at the Blackrobe, standing calmly.

The chief shrugged. "He says this is our god, too."

Tekakwitha stared at the Blackrobe, studying the cross on his chest. It was not just a cross, but held the body of a man. *Why should this horrible thing be the symbol of their god?* she wondered.

The chief looked to the women elders. They were the ones who decided important matters in the village. It was the women who appointed the chiefs, after all, who decided who was to be a slave and who was to be free; who would be part of the clan and who would not. They conferred in silence, exchanging only glances. After a long pause, they turned to the chief.

"If he wishes to build this chapel and teach us about his god," said her aunt, "then we should let him. We can always turn him away later."

The chief did not seem particularly pleased with this, but nodded his acceptance at the wisdom of the women. He turned to the Blackrobe and reluctantly gave his approval.

Almost immediately, the Blackrobe set about his odd tasks. The people of Gandawague gathered about his horses to watch him unpack. He took out rolled-up skins, books, a large cross, a metal goblet, and other unusual items, allowing the curious villagers to touch and examine them.

Tekakwitha stood apart, watching the others run their fingers over the drawings on the scrolled skins and the blankets. Once, the priest glanced at her, his eyes darting from scar to scar on her face. She lowered her eyes and quickly turned away.

I must go back to the maple trees. She moved toward the edge of the woods. Before she entered into its shadows, she looked back at the smiling Blackrobe surrounded by her people.

❖

The winter blew its chilly breath into the village, laying a blanket of white upon the wilderness, frosting the trees with a cold hand. The priest worked tirelessly felling trees and building a shelter, which he called a chapel. Its walls were built and its roof rose higher than the longhouses. Eventually, the Mohawks assisted the white man. Though spoke only French, some of the villagers understood him and they helped him haul the heavy logs from the forest and shared food with him during the long winter months.

When winter passed and the snows melted, making way for the timid greening of the forest, the chapel was close to completion. The priest invited the Mohawks to see it and began laying out his blankets and skins containing pictures, some of which the Mohawks understood, and many they did not. The priest, Father Pierron, began to use the pictures on the cloth to explain about his god.

Several warriors and women huddled together by the small fire in the chapel. Father Pierron played his "point to point" game on the blanket.

Tekakwitha watched from the doorway, her rabbit skin cloak over her head. She grasped the hood under her chin to keep the cold wind away. Father Pierron laughed with the people, trying to show them the picture talk. They laughed at the pictures, barely understanding. Tekakwitha watched the white man's fingers play over the blanket and over the brightly painted pictures that looked like her designs on breechclouts and skirts, and she slowly began to see what he was saying. She saw how the pictures began with birth, and how each event led to old age, and eventually to death. The pictures showed how a life can go on after death, how it soared like eagle's wings, and lived with Shonkwaia'tishon and the person on the cross.

Tekakwitha caught her breath and slipped from the doorway to lean against the outside wall of the chapel. She tightened her hold on her cloak. The cross again! What was it about the cross that so stirred her? The feelings were overwhelming, and suddenly she broke away, fleeing into the woods. The feeble warmth of the spring sun fell away beneath the cold shadows of the trees. The pine aroma was wet with lingering mist, and she found herself stopping at last, deep within the forest. Shafts of light angled down toward her, sending specks of leaf dust into the air. "The cross," she muttered. Why the cross? The others listened to the Blackrobe, but did not understand. When *she* listened, the sharpness of it rose up in her like ritual incense. Staying in the shadows, she had understood what the Blackrobe was saying to the others, though he never noticed her. She made certain of that. Always she kept to the edges of the crowd when listening to his strange talk, when he played his point to point game. Only occasionally, he looked up to see her. His eyes, so dark and strange, unsettled her, and she would move away from them once he observed her. His voice, though, was compelling, and she could not stop herself from listening to him each time he gathered the villagers to teach them about Jesus, the man on the cross. She wanted to know more, but it was difficult when Father Pierron could not speak their language.

One day, another Blackrobe arrived.

Tekakwitha sat outside the longhouse walls, the summer sun warming her dark hair. Some of the villagers took to helping the Blackrobe, Father Pierron, during the day and always her uncle would scowl at them, but he did not interfere. Tekakwitha tried not to think of the Blackrobe while she carefully stitched an elaborate design into a shirt. The colored beads and quills followed a spiral pattern, rolling and playing off one another just as autumn leaves chased and spun in the wind. Concentrating on her design, her fingers stitched a little cross. She gnarled her brows, staring at what she had done and brought the leather close to her face to examine her mistake. She could simply take the stitches out, and she poised her needle over the stitch to loop it under the thread to do just that...and hesitated. Perhaps a bead stitched into the center would hide her error. She lifted the garment once more, looking at the dark shape against the tan buckskin, before slowly lowering it to her lap. *Perhaps I shall leave it. What harm can it do?*

The villagers shouted and she jerked up her head to see what the commotion was. Riding into the center of the village between the longhouses and the creek, was another Blackrobe! Tekakwitha jumped to her feet and, forgetting the shirt in a heap on the ground, joined the throng that crowded round him. He raised his hands and declared loudly, "*She:kon, Riken:a!*"

The Iroquois gasped. The Blackrobe used their own language to greet them.

He dismounted and stood beside his chestnut horse, smiling at the crowd. Tekakwitha noted his shoulder-length reddish hair and the red hair under his nose and on his chin. She and the others saw French tappers with similar facial hair, but the Indians of the Iroquois Confederacy did not wear beards or mustaches. Mohawk men even shaved part of the hair on their heads, leaving something called a roach, much like a horse's mane running down the center from their forehead to the nape.

Father Pierron emerged from the chapel and greeted the other Blackrobe with an embrace. They spoke in French to each other for a long moment, and the words seemed to sadden Father Pierron. The other Blackrobe turned to the gathered Mohawks and gestured toward Father Pierron. "Father Pierron has served you well by building this fine chapel," he said in heavily accented Mohawk. "But now it is time for him to move on. I have come as his replacement. My name is Father Boniface."

At first, much time was spent helping Father Pierron pack his things. There was not enough time to get to know Father Boniface yet, but once farewells were said and Father Pierron's horses disappeared from view beneath the sheltering pines and elms, Father Boniface turned to the many Mohawks gathered. He met the chief who received him coolly.

"Now *you* wish to bring your god to us?" he said to Boniface at the feast they prepared in his honor. The chief's forehead was covered in ornamental red paint, and his hair sheened from bear grease. A single eagle feather dangled from his roach spread wider with porcupine quills. "Why do you need so many Blackrobes? Is not your god strong enough that he needs many to tell his story?"

Tekakwitha served at the feast, offering a large flat basket of shadberries and grassberries to the priest. He took a handful while looking up once at her scarred face, his eyes scouring it like the other priest had. "God is very powerful. He does not need me to tell his tale, but it is my desire to do so. Indeed, it is my duty, for I have dedicated my very life to him."

"I do not like the presence of Blackrobes in my village, but our treaty with the French says I must permit it, but only for so long. We are busy people. We are not idle like the French I have seen. You distract my people from their old ways. We have many festivals and much work to do before we celebrate them. Is it also your desire to take my people from the traditions of their ancestors?"

Tekakwitha recognized her uncle's tone. It was the same tone he used to challenge the other chiefs when they discussed deep matters. She squinted at the blurry white face of the Blackrobe, wondering if the priest could tell her uncle's dark mood by his voice.

Boniface's features grew serious and his lids covered his strange eyes for a moment, eyes the color of the sky. "Your traditions are important to your people. I should not like to change them. They are precious to you. But I would like to show you greater traditions and festivals. Festivals from which your people may learn new songs and music, for I know the Iroquois love their music."

The chief slowly nodded. "I will watch carefully what you do, Boniface. If I suspect you are trying to lead my people astray..." He leaned forward and said in a quiet voice, "I will not hesitate to kill you."

Tekakwitha shot a glance at the priest, whose eyes widened. Then a smile slowly teased at the edges of his mouth. "I believe you," he said calmly. "I will not lead them astray, but toward the Creator to know him better."

The chief sat back, leaning his elbow onto the soft pelts. His gaze did not leave the priest's face while he reached forward and took some dried venison, placed it between his even teeth, and tore it.

Tekakwitha finished serving and took her place not too far from the priest. Shyly, she glanced at his pale features, pleased with how he asserted himself with her stern uncle. Listening to his casual talk among the other diners, she resolved to attend to the priest as he talked to the others in the chapel. Her desire to know more about the cross grew stronger. The vision of that shape preyed on her mind, and she was certain it was a message from the Creator to her. Why else would Shonkwaia'tishon have brought these Blackrobes to Gandawague if she were not to learn more?

The next day when some younger Mohawks gathered in the chapel, Tekakwitha crept outside the window and sat down. She brought her sewing, plying her needle into the soft buckskin while her ears absorbed the Blackrobe's words.

The morning drew on, and Tekakwitha squinted at the chapel and then at the rising sun. "I cannot spend the entire day this way," she sighed, and rose, returning to her other duties. But much later, when the sun dipped behind the mountains and the sky drew on its dark blue mantle of stars, Tekakwitha moved back toward the chapel. With her rabbit skin cloak drawn up over her head and cinched tightly at her throat, she stood quietly in the doorway.

Alone, the priest knelt before a large crucifix with his head bowed. He resembled the medicine men when they gathered to speak to the spirits, with their fuming brands of juniper feathering smoke above their heads. At length, the priest rose, knelt on one knee to the cross, and abruptly turned to walk down the aisle...until he caught sight of her.

Tekakwitha ducked back out of the doorway, but it was too late.

"Don't be afraid," he called out to her.

She took a deep breath and pressed her nose to the doorway, allowing only one eyes to peer within the darkening depths of the chapel. The Blackrobe didn't move. His hand reached out to her, feet apart.

"I am not afraid," she said softly. Never before had she spoken to a Blackrobe. The notion was somehow exhilarating. She stepped into the doorway. The blanketing shadows fell over her, hiding her shyness. This time it was the priest's turn to squint at *her*. He could probably barely see her in the dim light, though this was the time of day that was easiest for Tekakwitha to see. The sun burned so brightly during the day it hurt her eyes. But now they did not ache from strain. She could look into the chapel and at the brightly burning candle flames and the cross, whose shadow flickered on the back wall. "The cross," she said, pointing. "I have seen it before. My mother…" Boldly, she took another step into the chapel, encouraged by Father Boniface's inability to see her clearly. "My mother said she was a Christian."

He blinked and gazed at her silently for a heartbeat before raising his hand to the cross hanging from his neck. "Did your mother speak of this?"

She shook her head. "No. She was afraid. She was a captive of my people. Made a slave. When my father met her, he made her a member of his clan. But she was not allowed to worship her god. She was afraid to speak of him to me. But when she especially feared, she held it tightly. What is it? Why is that man tortured on it?"

Boniface looked down at the cross in his hand. "This is not just a man. This is God."

Tekakwitha considered. There were great epic tales about many gods her people revered. But she could not recall hearing of any of the gods defeated, for then they would not be gods. "Why is your god tortured? He must not be a very powerful god."

"Oh, but he is! And infinitely kind. God loved us all so much, that he was distressed by our sin against each other and ourselves…"

"Sin," she said, drawing closer. "What is sin?"

Father Boniface tried to discern her features in the dark. She could tell he was trying to identify her by voice. "Sin is when we do something or say something which is cruel, unjust, or unkind. When we steal or murder."

"Or torture?" Tekakwitha stayed away from the festivals where captured enemies were presented. Often they were tortured, begging for death that finally came with a swift club to the head, or some other dishonorable end. She hated those times, when people she knew and loved, gentle people of gentle habits, somehow tossed their natures aside to commit unspeakable cruelty.

"Yes, or hurt anyone," the priest went on. "It separates us from the goodness of God. He wants us close, but when we sin we push ourselves away. And so, he sent his spirit to a maiden—like you— and asked her to bear his son, Jesus."

"And she did this?"

"Yes, she did. And this child—who is both God and man— grew to adulthood and grew very wise. He was without sin of any kind. Many of his followers wanted him to speak out and to call down violence upon the cruel leaders of their land, but he would not. He preached love. 'Love your neighbor as yourself' and 'love your enemy,' because we are all God's children."

"Not just white, then?"

"Oh, no. Mohawk, too. Oneida, Seneca, Onondaga—all the Iroquois. French and English, too. All. And because he loved us all so much, he offered to sacrifice his son, Jesus, to take away our many sins."

It was like a knife stabbing into her belly. The sensation was so real she reached down and clutched her stomach. Looking at the body on the cross, a feeling of horror overwhelmed her. She pointed with a shaky hand. "He suffered and died...for me?"

Boniface smiled. "Yes," he said slowly. "For you and for me. He took away our sins by his dying. And to prove that this was so, three days later, he rose from the dead."

Her fingers left her belly and rose to touch her trembling lips. "A ghost?"

"Not a ghost. He raised in body and spirit, and became proof of what awaits us all."

"We shall also become spirit and body?"

"Yes, someday. On the last day of the world."

"And you. A Blackrobe. Like Father Pierron. You travel and tell this story. Do many believe you?"

He smiled softly. "Oh, yes. All over the world. It is only here in the Iroquois longhouses that your people are beginning to learn of him. Even your own mother."

"But she did not tell this story. At least…well, it was so long ago. Perhaps I do not remember. Is it true?"

"It is. Blackrobes like me have come thousands of miles to speak of it, and they were willing to die for it. Many did."

"All for these two gods?"

"Oh, no, my dear. It is not two gods. One God, in three persons. The Father, the Son, and the Holy Spirit."

Tekakwitha cocked her head. "How can one god be three?"

"It is difficult, I know." He scratched his head, casting his glance about the dim room. Finally, he said, "The chief is father to his child, and uncle to his niece, as well as chief to his clan. Yet he is one man. He is three in one. You see?"

Tekakwitha breathed, absorbing his unfamiliar words but finding strange comfort from them. "Three in one," she whispered.

"We call it the Blessed Trinity."

"Trinity…" Tekakwitha rolled the word over in her mind, trying to grasp it, like a butterfly fluttering just beyond reach. How often was it so with Shonkwaia'tishon when she tried to understand his ways? Yet was this Blackrobe, this priest, not saying that Shonkwaia'tishon was this Trinity, a Father, a Son, and a Spirit? The notion took her breath away because it made so much sense to her, more than she imagined it could. "Are there no gods of corn?"

"No, child. Only one God."

"His name is Jesus."

"God the Father has no name. Indeed, the only one true God needs no name. His Son is called Jesus, a name given to the man born into the world. And the Holy Spirit is called just that."

"Father, Son, and Holy Spirit."

"Yes. And we bless ourselves with their holy names thus." The priest raised his hand to forehead and signed the shape of the cross across his body. Gently, Tekakwitha raised her hand and, following the example of the priest, signed herself.

"Am I blessed now?"

"Yes, you are very blessed. But you lack one of the most important blessings. That of baptism. We immerse ourselves in water to die to our old life and be washed clean, ready for our new life in Jesus, so we can live with him forever in Heaven."

"Do you have this water blessing?"

"I received my baptism when I was a baby. But you may receive it only after much learning. If you believe that Jesus is the Christ, the Messiah, sent by God to take away the sins of the world, if you come to believe he has done these things, then you, too must accept baptism so you will be a child of God."

A child of God…such strange ideas this priest has. Slowly, she pivoted on her heel. She walked toward the doorway, deep in thought. Turning back, she nodded in thanks, before slipping out the door.

She walked into the darkening night, mind full and heavy.

Fingers closed over her arm and she jumped in panic, a cry leaving her lips. She whirled, and gasped into her uncle's face.

"What are you doing in the white man's chapel?"

"I…I was only listening to the priest."

"Will you be like your mother? A slave because you are Christian? Only trouble can come of this. Leave it alone."

"But his words are full of truth."

"A white man's words? When have they ever been full of anything but lies?"

"He is not a trapper. He is a Blackrobe."

"Do I speak to the wind? Listen to me." He shook her arm in emphasis. "Only trouble can come of this. Leave it alone."

He released her. His silent glare told her the words he would not say, and he stomped away. Tekakwitha rubbed her wrist and slowly followed him into the night. But not before she looked back at the chapel and at the cross boldly standing atop its roof, sharp against the backdrop of stars.

CHAPTER THREE

Days later, Tekakwitha walked with her head held high, the wind slashing her dark hair across her scarred cheek. She closed her eyes, but even the protection of her lids could not prevent the sunlight from hurting. *But I do not care*, she offered to the wind. *Jesus of the cross; if you love me, too, I can bear this pain if only for a little while to feel the goodness of your sun and wind.*

Without fear, she pried open her taut lids. Sunlight streamed into her eyes and she shut them quickly again. But though the sun's strong light hurt her as much as it always had, she felt less troubled by the pain.

In the past, the shape of the cross puzzled, but not now. Knowledge of this Jesus who was God *and* man gave her new courage. "Perhaps my seeing this shape is a message. I did not understand before. Perhaps…I am no longer to be afraid of my pain."

She walked forward, lifting her face to the tall pine trees. Her ears filled with the sighs of the wind through the heavy boughs. Each prickly tree limb lifted and trembled with the wind's power, and they clashed with one another over her head, shadowing her path in dapples of fiery light and cool dark. "The wind is not a god," she said suddenly. And with such words, she caught her breath. She halted and felt her heart pound. She even raised a trembling hand to feel her heart beneath her buckskin poncho. "Not a god," she whispered.

She threw her chin forward and took off at a run toward the cornfields. Today, she did not walk carefully. It was no longer a dangerous path. Today, she rushed forward over the dead leaves of the forest floor, casting aside green fronds of glistening fern to reach the sunlight again and the greening fields of tall corn. She reached the field at last and threw herself between the rows. Its leaves cut her cheek, but she did not care. She cast her squinting eyes at the tall green stalks and the budding ears, their silk swaying in the chasing wind, a wind that seemed to chase her there.

She opened her arms to encompass the stalks, to smell their greenness, and she laughed, mocking the wind thrashing her hair about her face, blinding her more than the piercing sun. "There are no gods of corn!" she shouted, spinning in circles. The echo of her voice rebounded around her.

She pushed the stalks aside and ran toward the Mohawk River. Out of breath, lungs close to bursting, she reached the water and dropped to her knees on its stony banks. She cupped the cold liquid and cast up a fan of water, frightening a nearby trout, who darted away through the ripples in a flash of quicksilver.

"The river is not a god!" she shouted, throwing her head back. She laughed, until her laughter turned to confusion and the sudden release of tears. Her heart ached with love for this God she only just learned of, this God who was Shonkwaia'tishon and more. So much love she could not express it, even in her mind. Hot tears replaced the words and silvered her cheeks. "There is no god...but God," she said at last, an aching lump choking her throat. Silently, she watched the river's water coursing smoothly forward, foaming white around the hips of large rocks. A trout jumped, splashing the water with its landing and ducked into the waves, a dragonfly in its mouth.

She thought again of the cross and the figure of Jesus upon it, until her thoughts also turned to her uncle, who would not approve of such notions.

She wiped the tears from her cheek. "I must learn about Jesus." She said it to herself but also aloud so that the wind could hear. "If I learn enough, maybe Uncle could be made to understand. Even welcome it. And maybe I, too, can have the water blessing."

Idly, she dipped her hand into the river. "Water blessing." She slowly raised her wet hand to sign herself with the cross like the Blackrobe showed her.

"Tekakwitha!"

She whirled around at her aunt's voice and scrambled to her feet. "I am here," she said, raising her arm in greeting.

"Tekakwitha! All the time, I worry over you. And here you are sitting by the water. Child, I am always afraid you will stumble into it and be swept away."

"Do not fear that, Aunt." She brushed off her skirt and climbed the river bank. "God will protect me."

"'God'? That is a Blackrobe term. Should you not say 'Shonkwaia'tishon' instead?"

Startled that she had let that slip, Tekakwitha stopped and turned, measuring her aunt's mood by her posture. And just as the sun bursts over the mountain peaks, she knew her aunt's anger no longer mattered. "But they are one and the same, don't you see? I like the different ways of saying it."

Without waiting for the expected stinging reply, Tekakwitha hurried up the bank and back to the village.

Every day, Tekakwitha silently completed her chores. And after completing them, she found some excuse to walk near the chapel.

Inside, Father Boniface busily gathered with several Mohawks. He stood with his back to the altar and patiently taught them songs he also called prayers. The songs were different from that of their own festivals, for her people loved to sing and chant. These songs spoke of Jesus, the one also called Christ, and of the spirits called angels who serve him. She cocked her head and listened to the lyrical tunes climbing beyond the chapel's roof.

Though she yearned to, Tekakwitha never stayed too long. Her aunt watched her day and night. She did not wish to cause the Blackrobe any more trouble.

When winter came, Father Boniface asked some of the villagers to decorate the little chapel with pine boughs, feathers, and pinecones. At night, the small structure was alight with oil lamps, like little stars, and the sounds of singing could be heard all over the village. Even those who did no desire to go to the chapel favored the voices of singing children.

Tekakwitha sat in the longhouse chewing on dried otter meat, listening to the music climbing out of the wilderness. She found herself humming the now familiar tunes.

Her uncle shifted on his pelt and she raised her face to him. His frowned stopped her humming. "Why does the music displease you?" she ventured softly. "It is a good thing the Blackrobe brought to the village."

"Yes," said her aunt beside her, folding a robe she had just mended. "The children's singing has a very pleasing sound."

Her uncle only grunted and pulled a knife from its sheath and began to sharpen it on a whetstone.

Tekakwitha sighed, relaxing back into her own pelt, thinking of the next day. Father Boniface declared to the village he planned a special festival for everyone, something he called "Christmas." She tried not to show her eagerness, for she did not wish her uncle to forbid her to see it, but he, too, seemed caught up in the village's excitement and said he would see this Blackrobe festival for himself.

It began with many candles and oil lamps. So many Mohawks wished to see, that they crammed the little chapel and even perched in the windows. Father Boniface swung something like a metal gourd that smoked with a sweet-smelling scent, like spices and perfumes.

And then the singing began. The children's choir sang their songs of the Christ child and all listened, rapt, candlelight glowing on their upturned faces.

Tekakwitha nudged her way forward, staring at the little display before the altar. Small carved figures were set into a scene, and when Father Boniface spoke, she began to understand who they were.

First was the Holy Mother Mary, who knelt, gazing at her own child, the infant Jesus. Beside her stood her husband, Joseph. There were wise men from the East laden with gifts for the child as you would present to a chief. Above them perched a man with wings. Father Boniface said this was an angel, a messenger from God. All the figures were looking at the child. Father Boniface said he was a child born of humble and poor beginnings but grew to be the Savior of the world.

Tekakwitha gazed at the Jesus child. He lay in a wooden crib filled with straw, and his arms were outstretched, welcoming her. Even beyond the beautiful singing, the scent of incense, the golden lights flickering, the merriment of the others around her, she was drawn only to that sight of the beckoning child. Without realizing it, she had moved closer, enthralled by is mesmerizing face of innocence and wisdom. Arms wide, face impassive, the glass eyes stared back, and Tekakwitha suddenly yearned to be taken up in those small chubby arms.

When at last she raised her tear-filled eyes from the infant, her gaze rested on the crucifix above. The adult Jesus hung limply in death, those arms opened just as wide.

It was not long after that night that many Mohawks—both young and old—went to the priest and asked to learn about Jesus. They told him they wanted the water blessing.

Father Boniface was pleased, but he also appeared cautious. Tekakwitha knew he feared the chief, and bowed in greeting to him when he passed by the next day. But Tekakwitha's uncle, as always, scowled in reply.

Tekakwitha tended the fires for the maple syrup, but her mind was not on the large kettle, nor on the serenity of the woods. More than hearing Father Boniface's words in her head, she could *feel* them throughout her being. The woods themselves seemed alive with it, speaking in low tones about the Christ child, about the Trinity, and about Tekakwitha herself, though it was difficult to discern what exactly the words were. She leaned forward, listening.

Like her many waking dreams, she was silent and stiff, asleep but not asleep. Seeing and hearing the actions of God, she was drawn into an amazing vision that seemed to be truly happening. *Was* it happening? She drew closer, distancing herself from her body. Almost she heard the words, could feel them. If only she could draw even closer, hear them more clearly…

A whipping wind broke the moment. Looking up dazedly, she spied Father Boniface striding quickly by, arguing with a young Mohawk warrior.

"How can I turn the other cheek when my honor has been insulted?" cried the young man. "My people would never understand such a thing. I would be looked upon as weak. I would never be trusted again."

"But you must," insisted the priest. "If you love our Lord at all, you must give up some of those savage ways—"

"What you call 'savage' ways is how we defend our women and children. It has been so since Shonkwaia'tishon made the world and the People. Should we leave our villages defenseless to our enemies?"

"What I mean is that you must give up this warfare amongst your peoples. Love your enemies and make them friends, and we will all live under the peace of Christ."

"The gods protect me when I fight. Then I can come to this Jesus when I am old and at peace."

"No, no!" Boniface paced, digging a trench in the snow with his boots. "There are no gods! Why do you persist—"

The young warrior waved his hand dismissively. The shells on his long shirt and fur robe clicked softly together. "Your god makes no sense. He does not understand the needs of a warrior. I will not come again to your chapel. Teach the others. They are willing." With his long hair flapping over his shoulder, he left the priest and stalked back into the village.

Tekakwitha continued to stir her pot, though she did not breathe for some moments. The priest's face reddened before he expelled a hot breath that dissipated in a white cloud around his face. He cast a glance at Tekakwitha. "Your people can be…stubborn."

She nodded. "It is a gift."

Her studied her for a moment before the tension released from his shoulders and he laughed. "A gift? A gift, indeed. The Hebrew people, too, were stubborn and kept God's covenant throughout the ages. That was also a gift."

"I do not know of this Hebrew tribe," she said quietly, "but warriors can be particularly stubborn."

He shook his head. "He cannot seem to give up this notion of many gods. It is a blasphemy."

Tekakwitha stirred the pot. Its sweet-smelling steam rose, encircling her in its perfume. "There *are* no gods," she said simply.

Boniface studied her more carefully. "True. 'Worthless are all the false gods of the land. Accursed are all who delight in them.' I do not know you, do I? I do not think you are among those who have come to the chapel for instruction."

"No. I have not come. But I listen. The river is beautiful, but it is only a river. And the corn grows straight and tall, but in the end, it is still only corn. It is God who makes it grow."

"Yes." He stepped closer. "Who are you?"

She hid her face in the rising steam. "They call me Tekakwitha. My uncle is the chief."

"Oh, yes. I know you now. But you say you do not come to the chapel…"

"It is not safe for all of us to go, Father," she whispered.

He nodded and glanced over his shoulder toward the village.

"I must respect that, of course." He walked back into his footsteps in the snow and turned toward the village. Over his shoulder, he said, "But you are always welcome."

"I know. Christ's arms are always open." Shyly, she watched him depart, wishing she could speak more with him. "Shonkwaia'tishon, I feel you close beside me. You will tell me the time when I may go to the priest. Oh, I hope it is soon, I do not know how much longer I can bear to be closed off from your chapel and pray like the others do. But for now, speak to me in the wind like you always do and I will listen."

The wind suddenly cast back her cloak from her head and lifted her hair. The wind was cold on her cheek, but there was no discomfort in it. A song from the chapel choir rose in her mind, and she hummed the tune, rocking with its rhythm while she stirred the pot.

Her breathing slowed and her lids drew heavily over her eyes. The waking dream came upon her again and she saw Jesus and his arms outstretched on the cross. Then, in her mind, he was no longer on the cross, but standing and beckoning to her. Her lids pressed tight, squeezing forth a tear, and she gasped at the sight of Jesus, his love radiating outward. She lifted her arm, opening her fingers to his, almost touching. Her hand was different in this dream state. It did not seem to be her skin, but was instead radiant and glowing. She could not see her own face, but somehow knew it was as bright as her arm and no longer scarred. She was no longer herself.

The moment went on and on, keeping her suspended in that one rapturous instant. She was so deeply immersed, outside noises did not immediately register on her senses. It was a long moment later that she came back to herself. She paused to inhale, to wipe away the tears from her cheeks, and set the big stirring spoon aside.

A woman raced up the slope to the tree line and reached Tekakwitha with a gasp. "It is the great Kryn! Come, Tekakwitha. Come hear his stories!"

Tekakwitha's brushed aside the vision's lingering sensations.

She blinked and said nothing. The woman shook her head with irritation and retreated down the hill.

Clutching her cloak to her throat, Tekakwitha followed slowly. What had the woman said? She looked down the path toward the village and the gathering Mohawks.

The entire village converged on Kryn's horse. He dismounted and threw back his long black hair. The shells on his tunic were sewn into an intricate design, worthy of Tekakwitha herself. She knew of Kryn. He was once a great Mohawk warrior, but seldom did the others talk of him. One day he simply disappeared. They did not know what had happened to him. It was said he traveled very far over the great salty water. But others said that he took wives and began his own tribe further north.

He opened his arms to the people who gathered, and Tekakwitha gasped. On his chest hung a cross.

"My brothers," said Kryn. But then he spied Boniface and smiled broadly. He strode forward and embraced the priest, kissing him on both cheeks before holding him out at arm's length. "You are especially my brother," he said to the priest, who seemed taken aback by the greeting. "I heard of your great success in Gandawague. You baptized thirty Mohawks from this village alone."

"Why…yes. Forgive me, but I do not know you."

"I am Kryn, and I am Christian."

The crowd gasped, but Kryn turned to them. "My brothers, you have listened to the fine words of this Blackrobe and many came to know the truth of which he speaks. It is a wonderful truth, my brothers, because he speaks of God."

At last, the chief crossed the square and the tightly gathered crowd parted for him. He stopped before Kryn and eyed Father Boniface, before glaring at the cross on Kryn's chest.

Tekakwitha held her breath. Perhaps if her uncle accepted Kryn and his conversion, then it might be possible to broach the subject herself.

The chief raised his hand and pointed. "What is this you wear?

Is this not the symbol of the Blackrobes?"

"Not the Blackrobes alone, but of God."

"Which god? The Great Creator? This is not his symbol."

"It is the cross, the symbol of the crucified Christ, the Son of God and Savior of the world."

"The *son* of god?" The chief snorted and cast a glance to his fellow warriors. "This is the first sensible thing I have heard from these Blackrobes. Their god has a wife and son."

Kryn smiled. "This priest has been in your village all this time and you have not heard the stories of God the Father, the Son, and the Holy Spirit?"

The chief's face changed from indifference to anger. "How can you, a great Mohawk warrior, accept their Christian god?"

"My friend, once I heard the tale of him and his wonders, I could not ignore it."

The chief's eyes narrowed. "You speak like a fool. I did not know the great Kryn was a fool." The chief turned his back on Kryn and strode away.

The others hesitated, not knowing whether to follow their chief's example, until Tekakwitha's aunt pushed forward.

"Kryn," she said. "You are welcomed to Gandawague, even if my husband cannot tell you so himself," and she cast a backward glance at the retreating chief. "Christian or no," she said, eyeing his cross, "you are still a brother and it would be impolite not to take you into our longhouse."

Kryn smiled and put his arm around Boniface, following the chief's wife to the dwelling.

Kryn spent the entire afternoon talking of his adventures, punctuating them with stories of God's goodness to him. The chief would not speak to him, but many Mohawks, particularly those who were baptized by Father Boniface, were awed by what he said, especially when he spoke of the Sault Mission.

"It is a place to freely worship God," he said, the rich tones of his voice rumbling over the fires. "There, the Iroquois may pray all day if they wish, offering themselves in service to Jesus. We are surrounded with those of like minds, minds attuned to the Blessed Trinity." He cast a quick, undefined glance at the chief, who ate in silence and with eyes averted. "We need not worry that our beliefs will be mocked or that we will be in danger because of them."

The chief grunted but said nothing.

Tekakwitha closed her eyes and listened to Kryn's mellow voice. She tried to picture this mission, with its longhouses and chapel much like their own, tried to imagine people from all the Iroquois Confederacy working side by side and praying likewise in the chapel, Christian crosses on their chests.

The next morning when Kryn readied his horse, forty Mohawks stood silently around him. Already baptized, they waited with their families to go with Kryn to the mission.

Tekakwitha stood beside her uncle and watched the anger boil in his eyes, They stood at a distance from Kryn's party. "If they would go off on this foolish quest," he grumbled, "then let them. They are our clan no more."

Tekakwitha trembled. To be cast out of the clan was a serious matter. Yet even so, she longed to go with them. She knew it was the only way those who embraced the Christian faith would be safe.

Kryn approached the chief and raised his hand in friendship. "Peace, *Riken:a*. Your face speaks for your displeasure. I force no one to come with me. You could at least wish us well."

"Wish you well in this foolishness?"

Kryn lowered his face. "I am talking to the wind."

"Then let the wind listen to you. Be off, then. Take these clanless ones with you, if they will go. I will not stop them. But do not return here."

"We will go, *Riken:a*. I am sorry you do not understand. Perhaps someday you will." He turned from the chief to face Boniface. "Come with us, Father. Help these Children of God find their way."

Boniface agreed, and quickly packed his few belongings. Before mounting his horse, Boniface promised to return, glancing warily at the chief, who studiously looked in another direction.

With uncertain emotions, Tekakwitha watched them all ride out of the village. She would miss Father Boniface and his talks to the others. It would be a lonely time until their return, and even as their horses disappeared into the woods, and the last of the sounds of the Christian Mohawks singing hymns died away in the distance, she made her own way into the shadowy forest.

She took a silent moment to watch the dust shimmy down a shaft of sunlight before she sat on the soft blanket of dead leaves. Sighing heavily, she closed her eyes. *Jesus, Lord of all, why is it some are attuned to you, like the forty who left…and then myself? But some, like my uncle, refuse? Do you challenge them? Are they to know you in other ways? Why must faith be such a mystery?*

A gentle breeze—little more than a breath—lifted her hair and caressed her face with the dark strands. Understanding rose in her heart, and she felt the presence of the Creator just over her shoulder, the gentle breath of wind his own breath upon her. It made her aware of many things, but she could not share them, even with Father Boniface. These things God whispered to her seemed only for her own understanding, at least for the present. There might be time later to discuss these things with others but for now, she leaned into the sigh of wind, the rustle of the porcupine near his burrow, and the muddled chatter of finches high in the maple trees…and was at one with them.

Many months passed before Father Boniface returned. Tekakwitha noticed his pale features, the slow amble of his stride. "I do not think he is well," she said worriedly to her aunt one day, watching the priest make his way to the chapel.

After her words left her lips, Boniface suddenly collapsed. Nearby villagers rushed to him and took him into their longhouse. They nursed him with herbs and dancing prayers to the gods, but Boniface got no better. Tekakwitha watched from the doorway of the longhouse when he slipped into a deep sleep and never awakened.

Tekakwitha mourned the priest, praying for him to the Blessed Trinity, for she knew he would find the most delight in these prayers.

❖

The days grew longer. Tekakwitha felt them stretch into unceasing hours because the chapel was now silent. The baptized left with Kryn, and only she remained loyal to God but silent on the matter, waiting for something.

For the others, the days moved on as usual. Warriors made overtures to her uncle for her hand, but Tekakwitha always refused. Her aunts and friends watched with shaking head when she ventured into the woods alone. Sensing Tekakwitha was somehow different, the others began keeping their distance from her.

Tekakwitha could not explain to them what they refused to see, that God, the God of the Trinity, was everywhere and longed to welcome them all into His arms. Instead, she retreated further from village life, haunting the empty chapel.

Standing at the chapel's window, she peered inside into its gloomy interior The crucifix lay in shadow. The candles remained unlit. The darkness fell upon the dirt floor like a heavy cloak, silent and muffling. Despairing loneliness threatened to overwhelm her, until she lifted her eyes to heaven and whispered to the chapel's wooden walls, "Lord Jesus, give me comfort in my solitude. Here I am, surely your servant, but I don't know how to serve. Help me find the way." Her fingers delicately touched the bark still clinging to the chapel's walls, before she departed for her work, gathering pigweed and marsh elder.

Still thinking thoughts of the deserted chapel, Tekakwitha reached the meadow, and shielded her eyes from the bright sun. She followed her nose to find the bristly pigweed and pulled it from the soil and placed it in the flat basket she cradled at her hip. She thought of Father Pierron whose surprising entry to the village three years ago stirred everyone's emotions, and gave her her first glimpse of God, a presence she seemed already to know well. Then she thought of Father Boniface, who surprised Gandawague again by speaking their language, and baptized many Mohawks. "Oh, Lord," she sighed, "I remember Father Boniface saying that all we needed to do is ask you and we will receive. Lord of all, I am asking now. What must I do? What *can* I do?"

The rustle of the meadow grasses stirred her soul, for its breath seemed to be speaking to her, and she stopped, listening.

From the distance, she heard the gurgling sounds of a runlet, meandering its way to the Mohawk River. She smelled its water, sensed its fresh coolness, its purity while it ambled over stones and the flattened grasses of the meadow, nourishing the deer and rabbit when they paused before returning to their hiding places. "I, too, would be nourished with water." She closed her eyes, crushing tears of yearning. "I long for the water blessing of baptism. But how can this be, when there is no priest to do it, Lord?"

The deer raised its head, turning its huge ears in alarm. Suddenly, it sprinted toward the underbrush and vanished beneath the thickets. Tekakwitha raised her eyes toward the place the deer startled and smiled at such a benevolent God knowing it was the answer to her prayers.

Emerging from the dark forest into the meadow's sunlight, rode another Blackrobe.

CHAPTER FOUR

The village greeted Father Jacques de Lamberville warmly. Though all the Christian Mohawks had left with Kryn, there were others who were anxious to hear his message of God, and wondered aloud if they, too, should be Christian. At the urging of his wife, the chief reluctantly accepted this new priest, but he again warned the villagers against his strange and un-Mohawk customs.

Tekakwitha was eager to meet him. In her quiet ways she learned more about God and service to him than the others did listening to the priest in the chapel. But she knew there would come a time when she needed to speak with the priest and receive baptism. Tekakwitha felt called first to quiet paths before sitting at the feet of the priests and listening to their teaching.

Today, she neither walked nor sat in the chapel. Instead, she sat uncomfortably in the longhouse, her foot covered in a poultice. A day after the priest arrived, she stepped on a thorn and it soon festered. *I can be patient a little longer,* she told herself. *Soon I will talk to the priest and ask for baptism. Then all will be well.*

Sky Woman brought her a cup of willow bark tea. "Drink this. It will help the pain."

"No, thank you." Tekakwitha nestled more comfortably on the pelts. "My pain reminds me that Jesus suffered far more pain when he hung dying on the cross. Surely for his sake, I can endure a small discomfort."

Sky Woman glanced at Wild Flower and rolled her eyes, setting the tea down near Tekakwitha. They both sat beside her and picked up their mending.

Tekakwitha drew comfort from their company, their quiet sewing, even the little gossip they shared back and forth that became a soothing buzzing in her ear. But she knew she could not talk to them of her thoughts. Instead, she silently rocked her foot, her mind thinking of Jesus on the cross. It seemed right to suffer. Perhaps there was a way she could do more "penance" as the priest called it, this suffering in the name of God in order to pray for others. Perhaps fasting, give up some of her food, her raw hunger a reminder of the sacrifice given on the cross.

The longhouse door covering rustled. The Blackrobe, Father de Lamberville, poked in his head and looked around.

Tekakwitha sat up and watched the priest enter gingerly, greeting her aunt and the other women. "Forgive me this intrusion," he said, bowing to her, "but I was walking by, and I felt the need to step inside to...to..." He shook his head, smiling at his own foolishness. "Truly, I do not know. I go where the Lord leads me."

Her aunt snorted the same disdainful sound the chief made toward Blackrobes. She glanced at Tekakwitha to share in this joke, but Tekakwitha was enthralled that the priest should come into her longhouse uninvited.

De Lamberville's eyes followed the aunt's gaze to Tekakwitha and he half smiled at her as he slowly approached. The other women looked up mildly.

"Did you hurt your foot?" he asked.

Tekakwitha nodded. "Yesterday. I stepped on a thorn. I do not see well."

De Lamberville crouched beside her to be at eye level. He was thin, with pale freckles on his face and hands. His hair was a light brown and his eyes were gray like a winter morning mist off the creek.

Her gaze fell from his face to the cross hanging over his broad white collar. "My mother wore a cross like that."

Startled, de Lamberville studied her. "Indeed? Was your mother Christian?"

"Yes. She was Algonquin, captured by the Mohawks." She glanced quickly at the two women resettling themselves uncomfortably. "She was made a member of the Turtle Clan and married my father the chief. But that was so long ago. I scarcely remember her, and she did not tell me of the Christian faith. It took a long time, but I, too, Father, want to be baptized. I want to belong to Jesus."

The gray eyes widened. "Who are you?"

"I am Tekakwitha, niece of the chief of Gandawague."

De Lamberville paused. Tekakwitha knew the chief had spoken harshly to the Blackrobe and to the other priests, even threatening them. To baptize the niece of the chief would surely put this man's life in danger. Seeing all this in his face, she gently touched his hand. "I know what my uncle said to you. But don't be afraid. God will protect you."

A corner of his mouth flickered briefly, though his brows frowned. "What do you know of God, Tekakwitha?"

"I know that he is one in three persons. The Father, the Son, and the Holy Spirit. I know that God the Son died on the cross many years ago for our sins, both the sins of the past and those future generations. I know that he loves us with a burning love, and that he did this to save us from the powers of Satan so we can live in love with one another. He did it for me and for you, and I know that you have come to spread this good news of the Gospel."

The priest's lips parted but no words came. He glanced at the other women whose faces scowled deeper the more Tekakwitha spoke. "How do you know this? Did Father Boniface teach you?"

Tekakwitha smiled. "No. I did not take lessons from Father Boniface, but often I listened to him from outside the chapel. And every day—sometimes during much of it—I pray. I listen to the sounds of the birds when they wing. I listen to the water in the Mohawk rushing to its secret places. I listen when the wind moves the cornstalks. I see what God does for us, making corn grow tall, entwining the stalks with bean vines, and growing the bright green squash from a yellow blossom. If you are quiet, Father, and very still, God will speak to you in these things. He will instruct you."

For a long moment, the priest stared at her. Slowly, he lifted his hand and passed it over his mouth. "My child," he whispered, his voice trembling. He opened his mouth to speak, but seemed to change his mind. Just as quickly, his faced changed again and he stood. He glanced at Tekakwitha's aunt. "You...you still have much to learn. Certainly you will be baptized, but it cannot be soon. You may not be ready."

A dart of disappointment jabbed her heart, but Tekakwitha offered the priest a dignified smiled. "Of course, Father. When you think I am ready."

"You must come to the chapel for further instruction. Listening at windows is not enough."

She nodded. "Anything you ask of me, Father, I will do."

Tekakwitha felt suddenly at peace. Even though the priest delayed her baptism, it didn't seem to matter. It was going to happen, and now she was anxious for her foot to recover so she could get to the chapel.

A shadow fell over her and she glanced up at the worried expression on her aunt's face. "You must speak to your uncle of this."

The expected fear was not in her heart, and Tekakwitha offered her aunt a smile. "When he returns, I will do so."

Later that day when the chief did return, he sat heavily beside her, the beads and shells of his shirt clicking together. His weathered face glanced once at the guilty expression of her aunt before turning his gaze on Tekakwitha. The red paint under his eyes and along his nose gave his face a kindly appearance, even though his eyes were angry. "I will hear it from you," he said.

She took a deep breath and thought a quick prayer for help. "I told the Blackrobe that I wish to be Christian like my mother. I have been thinking about it a long time, Uncle. Many years now, in fact. I don't do this lightly. I believe in God. I believe his Son died on the cross for us. I believe in everlasting life in Heaven."

"These things are for white men, not for us. Tekakwitha..." His changing features made him look suddenly old. She noticed his gray streaks in his braided roach, the lines running down his cheeks and how the paint caught in them. "These things are not for us."

"It is for me, Uncle. And—forgive me—but you are wrong. It is for all of us."

"No. Not this. Tekakwitha, think of your position in the village. If you become Christian, no one will want to marry you."

With a sigh, she spoke the words she knew would deeply disappointment him. "Uncle, I do not wish to *ever* marry."

"Now I *know* this is all nonsense!" He tore the little tobacco pouch at his sash and threw it down. It lay on the pelts like a dead thing, tobacco leaves spilling out. "You see where this Christianity leads you? This is not Mohawk. A maiden marries and bears sons. She does not dedicate her life to her maidenhood. It is a disgrace. Would you be a pauper?"

"I am not afraid of poverty. All I need is a little food, a few pieces of clothing."

"Poverty, eh? More than that. The disgust of all that know and respect you. This god you say you love asks too much from you."

"He did not ask it of me. I give it."

"You give away your heritage? You give away yourself?"

His anger was like a heavy cloak about him. Once, it made her cringe with its fierceness, like facing down a badger protecting its burrow. But today, it seemed only to be a distant thing, something not to be feared, but pitied. *Such anger and such hatred,* she mused. *It breeds nothing but more discontent. It makes nothing useful. It does not plant or reap. It creates no longhouse, nor corn cake to eat. It does not sew a cloak to keep out the chill. Strange how I never noticed this before.* And then she considered her uncle's words. To him, to "give herself away" was a terrible thing, to be Mohawk no more. But to Tekakwitha, the notion took hold of her with sudden immense importance. "I give myself away," she said thoughtfully. "Yes, Uncle. That is, indeed, what I am doing. I am giving myself away and becoming…more."

"How can you be less and be more?"

"Because I am less Tekakwitha and more in God."

Her uncle cast his gaze in search of a reply. When none came, he made a sound of disgust and threw his hands in the air. Before he stalked away from her, he glared at her two companions Sky Woman and Wild Flower, who suddenly did not find their association with her to their liking. The women, too rose, and left her alone.

Tekakwitha watched them go with a slight nod. "I do understand," she said to herself. "You must be on his side. It is the safer place to be. But I will stay on God's side, for it is the *better* place to be."

Daily, Tekakwitha went to the chapel and instead of hiding in its shadows, walked proudly through the front door. She bowed her head in acknowledgement to the priest when he looked her way. She stilled herself while he taught, keeping her eyes lowered and listening. Sometimes she closed them completely, not because of the pain the light caused her, but to immerse herself in the priest's words while he spoke of Jesus, his parables, his wisdom, his love, his ultimate sacrifice, and of his glorious and amazing resurrection.

"Tekakwitha," he said gently for the second time.

She opened her eyes and noticed his bending over her. His expression was one of impatience.

"I'm listening, Father de Lamberville," she said quietly.

"I asked what you could tell me about the Holy Eucharist."

"It is the body of Christ himself," she answered simply.

He turned to walk up the aisle. The rustle of his woolen robes released a hint of incense. "Is it the symbol of his body, then?"

"Oh, no," she said, interrupting a young Mohawk about to make an observation.

De Lamberville turned to her and quietly motioned for the other to sit. "Tell me, then. What proof have you?"

"The proof is in the Scriptures, Father. It was at the Last Supper. Jesus told his followers the Apostles that they were to take the bread and eat; 'For this is my body,' he said. And when he picked up the cup, he told them, 'This is my blood of the new covenant which will be shed for you. Do this in remembrance of me.' But that is not all."

"No?" De Lamberville observed her curiously, an expression of expectation on his face.

"He also said in the Gospel of John that we must eat his flesh and drink his blood or there would be no life within us. At the Last Supper, he explained how this could be so."

"And how is it so?"

"A priest—like yourself—is endowed with the spirit of God to change the simple bread and wine into the body and blood of Christ at the Mass. It is…" She searched her mind for more words, but at last gave up and shrugged. "It is a mystery just how it is done. But we have faith that it *is* done because our Lord told us it would be."

De Lamberville gazed at the others in the room. He wanted to say more, but he shut his lips instead and nodded silently. "Well said." He walked up the aisle to the sanctuary where he stood a long time, contemplating the crucifix.

"You are all excused for the day," he said to the class of five Mohawks. He did not turn when they left their benches, scattering dust their moccasins kicked up from the floor. Once all was quiet, he slowly pivoted on his heel, and did not seem surprised to see Tekakwitha still at her spot. He breathed slowly before walking down the aisle. For another several heartbeats, he stood above her, saying nothing. She thought that perhaps he was waiting for her to look up.

"Father?" she asked.

"Always you are the first here, and always you are the last to leave. What is it you seek, Tekakwitha?"

"I have already found it, Father?"

He glanced at the crucifix, shadowed by the late afternoon sun. Only the face of Jesus was illuminated by the golden light. Though the carver depicted a Jesus who died, the radiance of the sunlight on his gentle features enlivened it. At any moment, the carved eyes seemed prepared to open. De Lamberville unaccountably shivered.

"Child, what do you ask of God?"

Still looking up at the priest, Tekakwitha pried opened her eyes despite the pain. "To deepen my faith and open my heart to his people."

He nodded. "What does faith offer you?"

She smiled. "Life eternal, where there is no sickness, no pain, no hate. Only love."

"And what do you ask of God's Church?"

"To be baptized and to receive the body of Christ. I wish this with all my heart, Father."

Looking at her intently, Father de Lamberville lowered beside her, balancing on the balls of his feet. "Child, you know how your uncle feels."

"Yes, I know. All the village knows."

"Then you must realize how your life will change."

Tekakwitha searched the priest's freckled face, the worry lines slashing across his forehead and the wrinkles at the corners of his eyes "When you entered God's Church as a priest, did your life change?"

"Yes. Very much so. But that is different—"

"Is it? You have made a vow of chastity and poverty because you love God. Why should it be so different for me?"

He took a deep breath and placed his hand on his heart. "You humble me, child. Sometimes I have little faith in the courage and spirit of those I baptize here in the wilderness. I forget that God reaches each of us in his own way. It is difficult to remember this." He smiled but quickly sobered. "If you are willing to take the risks, I will baptize you this coming Easter. In one cycle of the moon."

Tekakwitha could not breathe. For a moment, all time seemed

to stop. The breeze which fluttered the priest's hair seemed to hang in space, moving very slowly. The specks of dust shimmering in a beam of sunlight slowed to a crawl, and even a mouse skittering along the far wall stopped to contemplate the priest's words. To be baptized! To receive the water blessing at last! The blessing that would take away her sins and join her into the family of Christ!

For a month, Tekakwitha walked on air. She did her customary chores and after, went along into the woods to pray, kneeling on the fragrant pine boughs in a forest bursting with the first notes of spring. Ferns slowly reached upward with their green curled arms, not yet willing to open their fan leaves, flower buds poked through the soil alongside mushrooms with their brown caps. Squirrels came out of hiding. So did the rabbit and fox. Everywhere was the evidence of renewal, of life starting again. And for Tekakwitha, she knew her life, too, would a start anew with her baptism the next day.

Early in the morning, well before the sun rose, Tekakwitha slowly dressed in her freshest buckskin. Carefully, she ran bear grease into her hair before braiding it, and tied a beaded headband around her forehead, draping its feather to the side over one ear. She decided not to put paint on her face this day, knowing the water and oil of baptism would be enough. Then, looking around at the sleeping figures gray in the darkness, Tekakwitha pulled the small cross out from under her sleeping furs. She made it from sticks tied with sinew, and likewise its necklace from tiny shells strung together with dried otter tendon. She put this over her head and laid the cross lovingly own her chest.

"This is a mistake."

The voice did not startle her this time. She suspected her uncle would be awake early on this day of all days. "It is not a mistake," she replied.

"Yes. Just like your mother. A slave."

"She was not a slave after my father married her."

"But she was not free to be Christian either. Just as you shall not."

"Uncle—"

"Tekakwitha!" He grabbed her hair, yanking a braid downward. She was painfully forced to look up at him. "Because of your rank in this village, you have known privilege. And you lived up to the respect you were given. But you take these things too lightly. We will not accept your Christianity. We will not allow you to retain your rank. You will know poverty even though you scorn me for telling you so. You are a young woman of twenty summers. In twenty more, you will be sorry for your decision not to marry. No sons will hunt for you. No daughters will care for you with medicines when you are ill. Look at you. Always unwell since the white man's sickness took your family and my brother. And now you join them in their religion. You should be treated no better than a slave for your ingratitude." He released her, tossing the braid aside. He glared while she rubbed her head. "I warn you. Do not go through with this. You will have no place in this longhouse if you do."

She nodded, understanding his hurt. Softly, she said, "I will not give this up. It has been my heart's desire for longer than I knew Jesus. I was drawn to him. I am still drawn to him. This you cannot stop, even if you kill me, and that is what you shall have to do to stop me."

Rising, she straightened out her skirt and poncho top, affixing the cross in the center again.

"If you do this you will surely influence others."

"I know. That is my hope."

He stood behind her. She heard the faintest of sounds issuing amid the snoring and the wind flapping the longhouse's hide walls. It was the sound of a knife drawn from its leather sheath. She felt the shadow of her uncle approach, felt the tingle of his nearness run down her spin. Tekakwitha held her breath. If he intended to kill her, her only regret was that it was before her baptism. She hoped that Jesus would receive her anyway into Heaven.

She closed her eyes and prayed.

A moment passed, and then another. Clumsily, her uncle

slapped the blade back into its sheath and grunted. He turned from her and stalked from the longhouse.

She prayed a prayer of gratitude for being spared for this day, and rose to make her way to the chapel.

The chapel was ablaze in light. Some Mohawks were already there, anxious to watch the proceedings. Tekakwitha heard the whispers. She knew what the talk was; how strange they thought her for spending so much time alone, with no interest in finding a husband. Yet all that did not matter. The murmurs faded into the background, the faces blending with the colors of the spring flowers, feathers, and ribbons around the altar. Tekakwitha felt herself swept away to a far place, with the shining face of God smiling down on her. "My lord and my God," she whispered, not even realizing when she stood before Father de Lamberville.

Garbed in white, he seemed to glow. The sweet scent of incense filled her head and permeated the close air of the chapel. From a distance, she heard his words softly intoned, and felt the cold water of the font run down her forehead.

"You are a new creation," he said into her ear...or was it the voice of God? "Your new name is Kateri. May you wear the name of this holy saint faithfully while you follow our Lord Jesus Christ."

"Kateri," she mouthed. She walked slowly back down the aisle, sensing not the earth beneath her moccasins, but downy clouds. All around her, the feathers and ribbons hanging on the walls fluttered from an unseen wind, undulating together like the long grasses in a meadow, forming and reforming as ever the shape of the cross. "I understand, Lord," she said breathlessly. "I understand."

It was the last time she wore moccasins.

CHAPTER FIVE

Kateri's buckskin dress was soiled, but there were no others to change into. She braided her hair neatly, but without bear grease, and she no longer painted her face. Her toes were dirty and blue with bruises. The soles of her feet were scraped and crusted with old blood. A bruise still colored her arm where the stone had landed, but she no longer felt its dull ache. That was only yesterday. But the week before, a warrior had threatened her. She had ignored him and walked away, but a woman nearby had picked up a rock and threw it at her. It happened more often now. She tried to keep herself, but it was difficult.

Though she still shared the same longhouse with her uncle, she was not welcomed to his cooking fire. She kept to herself, often with no fire at all. Yet every sunup, she retreated to what she called her sacred places in the woods, the places where she carved a cross on the tree's bark, and knelt to pray. It was the quietest then, when the air was still, resting on a rosy tint above the hills. Only the occasional sound of someone chopping kindling echoed back to her from the river's edge, or the sound of an early bird beginning its song. But even though she meditated in solitude, she knew she was not alone.

"Blessed Trinity," she said, "I give you thanks for the blessings of my life, for reaching down to find me here. Blessed Jesus, I hope my small sufferings can be solace to you for what you endured for the life of the world. May I never be a source of woe to you or to the Father. I pray that my sufferings may bring my soul a joyful gaze upon you, O God."

Her knees began to ache, but still she knelt. Food and rest were far from her thoughts. Ever since her baptism, Kateri felt different. "A new creation," Father de Lamberville told her. No longer Tekakwitha—the one who stumbles, but now Kateri, named for Saint Catherine of Siena, who also chose to live a life of celibacy. She, too, lived in ill health for most of her brief life, and cared for those others ailing more than she, even victims of plague. Kateri never forgot to thank her patron for such an example of devotion. "There is a reason Father de Lamberville named me so," she said. She lifted her face to a bird high in a pine tree and closed her eyes to listen to its sharp call.

For a long time, she merely listened to the birds, the hot August wind rustling the pine needles, and then to the sounds of the village awakening, before she finally rose. She stretched her back and walked slowly, mindful of the stones, and neared her water jar just when Sky Woman emerged from the longhouse. She did not make her accustomed greeting to Kateri but stood instead with a hand at her hip and her head tilted insolently. She made no move to help while Kateri lifted the empty jar to her head.

"So," said Sky Woman at last. "The Christian comes to do her chores. I thought they were too good for you, these Mohawk ways of ours. Christians live a different life."

Kateri said nothing when she turned toward the stream. The air was already growing oppressive from the summer heat and humidity, and Kateri was anxious to get to the water, but Sky Woman grabbed her arm and the empty water jar toppled from Kateri's head, shattering on the ground.

"Tekakwitha, you are as clumsy as always. Look what you have done."

Kateri glanced mildly at the shards. "My name is no longer

'Tekakwitha.' It is Kateri."

"'Kateri'? What sort of name is that? A Christian name?"

"Yes. Named for a saintly woman."

"Do you think because you are now Christian you are a saint, too? You make me laugh, Tekakwitha." With a snort, Sky Woman crossed in front of Kateri, kicking a jagged shard at her, before looking tauntingly back over her shoulder.

Kateri measured the shards on the ground, and one by one, picked them up to take to the discard pile of broken pots and torn baskets. Out of the debris, she retrieved a cracked jar and put that on her head to take to the river.

"See the Christian who digs in the trash like a dog," said Wild Flower, a bundle of sticks tucked under her arm.

"My jar was shattered. I needed another. This one is still good."

"It is the home of spiders. I suppose that is now where you belong, Tekakwitha."

"Why do you curse what you don't understand? If you knew the happiness I have in my Lord, you would not scoff at me."

"This is happiness? The leavings of others? Your broken body and bloody feet? You look like a rag doll, Tekakwitha. Is it worth it?"

"My name is Kateri."

"I don't recognize such a name."

"It is my Christian name. It is my name now."

Wild Flower stared before her mouth drew down. "You are not a Mohawk."

"But I am."

"No! You spit on our ways. You go alone to your 'prayers.' You do not help with the work of the women, and you look like a slave. The chief should have killed the first Blackrobes who came here."

"Just because your brother became Christian and left with Kryn, do not be angry at me."

Kateri was not prepared for the slap to her face. It burned her cheek and jerked back her head with its terrible force. Her ears rang with it, and without thinking, she raised her hand to the hot welt.

Wild Flower glowered. "You will not speak of him. He is dead."

"No. He is more alive than before!"

A slap again, and again Kateri's ears rang.

"You are worse than a slave, Christian! You are not Mohawk." Her eyes glittered, daring Kateri to speak, but Kateri only gazed at her kindly before turning away.

Her bare feet walked carefully over a grassy verge sloping downward toward the river's edge. The stony beach, strewn with palm-sized rocks smoothed into ovals and globes, chuckled under her steps. In her head, Kateri spoke the words of a Psalm and found comfort in the spirit of it, written so many years ago. *"For your sake I bear insult, shame covers my face. I have become an outcast to my kin, a stranger to my mother's children. Because zeal for your house consumes me, I am scorned by those who scorn you."*

She dipped the pot into the creek and watched its clear waters rush in to fill it. *"See you lowly ones, and be glad; you who seek God, take heart! For the Lord hears the poor, does not spur those in bondage. Let the heavens and the earth sing praise, the seas and whatever moves in them!"* She withdrew the dripping jar, but before placing it on her head, spied a figure couching upstream. Because of her sight, she could not tell who it was, and squinted in vain trying to discern features. All she saw was a blurry face turn toward her. At that distance, she could not even tell whether the figure was a man or a woman.

Something inside her made her approach. She stepped with care over the slippery stones. Soon she was close enough to note a canoe bobbing against the current and scraping along the shore. The figure was obviously a man, but one she did not recognize. He rose slowly.

"You wear a cross," he said, his voice deep and even.

The cracked jar on her head weeped into her hair and trickled over her dim eyes. Any natural caution fled from her and she stood fixed, her skirt whipping in the persistent wind. "I am Christian. My name is Kateri."

"Kateri…" He wiped the water from his lips with the back of a

47

large hand. "You have scars on your face. Old scars from long ago." The black paint across his eyes made them more readable to her bad eyesight. Their expression seemed tender. "I am Garonhiague. I use no saint's name, but I am Christian, too."

"Where do you come from?"

"From the Oneida. I am a chief. Or, at least...I was."

"Were you cast out because you are Catholic?"

"No. I chose to stay away from the longhouses. I live with my wife at the Sault Mission. I was on my way to visit my tribe and my relatives, but I will return to the mission when I am done."

"I see." Kateri lowered her face and made to turn up the slope. "I wish you well and God's blessing, then."

Garonhiague moved forward and reached, but not touch her. "You find it easy, then, to live the life of a Christian in this village?"

She hesitated. Water sloshed from the jar and splattered in the dust. Garonhiague looked down and noticed her bare and bruised feet. "I have never found my life to be particularly easy."

"They accept you, then?"

Kateri pressed her lips tightly. "No. None of them do."

He smiled. Now she noticed a bit of red paint smeared down his chin from under his lower lip. "I am glad you did not lie, for I heard what that woman said to you."

"We used to share a longhouse."

He gestured to her feet with a frown. "So they force you to live like a slave, even taking your moccasins from you?"

She shook her head. "I chose to live this way. It is in remembrance of the sufferings of our Lord."

He nodded slowly. "Have you a priest here? I would see him."

"Yes. I will take you to him."

Kateri climbed the embankment and Garonhiague followed a few paces before two more Indian men emerged from the cottonwoods. Kateri said nothing while the three followed her to the chapel.

She left the water jar at the doorway and entered, becrossing herself in the sight of the crucifix. "Father de Lamberville. These are friends and they wish to see you."

"Garonhiague!" De Lamberville rushed forward and embraced the Oneida chief, kissing him on both cheeks. "I have not seen you in many years."

"I travel much and talk about the Catholic faith."

The other men moved forward and Kateri backed away toward the threshold. Men needed their chance to talk, and she wanted to go back to the woods to pray.

"Wait, Kateri. These men are old friends of mine. They live at the Sault Mission."

Kateri smiled in polite acknowledgement.

"You do not wish to hear of the Sault Mission?" asked Garonhiague's taller companion, a Huron.

"Forgive me. I have heard of the Sault Mission, and many from this village already went there. I remain here. My uncle the chief will never let me go."

"Your uncle is the chief?" asked the other man. He was shorter and broader than the other two, with black paint streaked down his long nose. His roach was braided with several red-striped hawk feathers. "Are you of the Turtle Clan?"

"Yes. My father was the chief. He married an Algonquin Christian. But they have both been dead for many years."

"I am your mother's cousin, then. You must be the one called Tekakwitha."

"I am Kateri now."

He smiled and turned toward the priest. "She is my relative."

But de Lamberville was looking at Kateri, his forehead stepped with lines. "It has not been easy for her here. Yet she does not complain."

Kateri held his gaze and did not waver, even when he could no longer look into her eyes.

"I fear for her," he went on. "She is threatened almost daily. It has been worse for her than for the others. She has an important position in the tribe."

"Have you no husband to protect you?" asked Garonhiague.

"No husband," she said softly. "Not ever."

Garonhiague's brows rose. "I see."

"I see no other way for her," said de Lamberville. "And she is a precious treasure."

"Many are loyal to our Lord," reminded the Oneida.

"Yes, but none are like this one."

Kateri did not blush at such words, for she did not hear them. She stopped listening, and their voices blended into the background of creaking wood and flapping hides. The sight of the crucifix drew her quickly into a deep meditation. Its cross burned a dark image into her eyes, with light blazing in a corona about its dark contours. Jesus opened his eyes and gazed at her tenderly, and again, in her dream state, she reached up to him. So close, their fingers almost touched...

"Kateri," said de Lamberville. "I think it the only thing to do."

"What is?" she asked dreamily, not yet fully aware of them.

De Lamberville grasped her shoulders and stared into her eyes. "Kateri! You must go with Garonhiague to the Sault Mission. It is the only safe place for you. You must not return here. I think if you stay longer...someone will kill you."

"I will gladly die for my Lord."

"I know you would willingly," he said. "But there is something special about you, Kateri. You can be so much more to so many more, and live as you desire at the Sault Mission. There are many ways to serve the Lord. I insist you go."

"What of my uncle?"

"Hang your uncle!" Awakened at last by de Lamberville's tone, Kateri's eyes widened. The priest smiled sheepishly. "I mean to say...that we cannot rely on your uncle's counsel any longer. You must go with these men now while your uncle is away at the fort."

Kateri looked from one anxious face to the other. It was not only her own life she risked, but now these others. No one ever did such a thing without the chief's permission. *Uncle would never permit it...*

Suddenly her heart began to beat like a festival drum, pounding faster and faster. To live at the mission! To pray! To love and honor God! The words of the Holy Mother rose in her mind, crying out with a young girl's hopeful innocence: *My soul proclaims the greatness of the Lord; my spirit rejoices in God my savior.*

Her heart filled with the love of God. *Do not be afraid*, the Scriptures said, and she wasn't. Kateri gazed contentedly at each man before she smiled. "I will go with you."

De Lamberville grew stoic. "Get whatever you need now. They will await you at the river." She was in a waking dream again, lifted by unseen hands and ushered out of the chapel. Vaguely, she heard the priest say to the men while she rushed over the threshold, "I will write a letter for you to take to the mission."

Her feet slapped the dusty ground, casting up little clouds behind her. She reached the longhouse and found her place by the cold fire ring. Taking up a pouch, she stuffed in her winter fur cap, her needles, her winter cloak, and some dried meats and dried currants and corn. She looked at the wampum necklaces she owned and decided to put those on, but left the tobacco pouch and other wampum bracelets. Lastly, she rolled up her blanket and tucked it under her arm and looked about the familiar longhouse. "For all my life you were a home for me," she said to the walls of sticks and hides. Inhaling, she sighed and with it, the ache in her soul. "But you were never truly my home. Now, I think, I *am* going home."

With no one to see her, no one to question her, Kateri made her way to the river where the Huron and her cousin the Algonquin waited by their canoe.

CHAPTER SIX

Slowly—it seemed so slowly—the canoe speared the water. Each man dipped in his oar and stroked the river, coaxing the bark canoe farther away from Gandawague.

Kateri wished the Oneida chief Garonhiague was with them. He was so confident, so reassuring. But he told the others he must first fulfill his obligations to see his tribe. He said he would join them later, but his absence made Kateri uneasy. She hugged her arms though she was not cold.

The muscles on the Huron's arms bunched and relaxed when he pushed the oar. Kateri sat straight and still, watching the shore whiz by them in a blur of green. Crouching at the bottom of the canoe, she pressed her pouch against her hip. The paper from Father de Lamberville crackled softly inside. She wondered what the letter said. He told her it was for the priest of the mission. Since she could not read the white man's writing, her vague curiosity at this strange paper would have to wait to be satisfied only when she reached the mission. But when would that be?

Her cousin the Algonquin turned to her just then, sweat running down the painted ridge of his nose. One corner of his mouth rose briefly in encouragement before he turned back to the work at hand, but she was little reassured. She wanted to be much farther away. Who know when her uncle would return and hear of her flight? What would happen then?

The afternoon fled. Kateri sat on the shore and watched the shadows of the cottonwoods reach into the stream, drawing the river's colors of tawny brown, green, and ice blue, into darker tones, speckled by fallen yellow leaves. Gnats circled the places on the shore that smelled of rotting algae.

"When will he be back?" she asked her Algonquin cousin.

The Algonquin scanned the opposite shore before sitting beside her. "It won't be long. The settlement is not far. We were in such a hurry to get your from your village that we did not gather provisions. But all will be well."

Kateri pulled the pouch at her hip forward and reached inside. "Here. Share what I have."

He looked down at the meager amount of dried meat and berries. Smiling, he shook his head. "No, thank you. He will return soon. Keep it."

She looked back toward the bend in the river. Never having traveled this far before, she was uncertain exactly where she was. It occurred to her that she did not know how far the mission was either. "I know the mission is far away…"

"Farther than you know." He sat back, leaning on his elbows and stretching his long legs forward. His wampum beads clicked against the bare skin of his chest. "It will take us two moon cycles to get there."

"That long?"

"That far," he said and smiled.

She smiled back until he leaned forward with a curious expression. He indicated her face with an index finger. "These scars. What are they?"

Kateri gazed over the water, squinting at the bright reflections. "When I was a child, the white man's sickness came to the village. We all got sick, including my family. My father the chief died first. I remember him being so big and so strong. But he died. It was so terrible. And then my baby brother, not even a year old, died. And finally my mother. She never did tell me about Jesus and Heaven. I wish she had. I would not have wept for them so much, knowing I would see them again."

"And you? Were you the only one to survive the sickness?"

"There were others, but not many. It left me weak, barely able to see, and scarred."

The Algonquin gazed out to the river. His jaw tightened. "Kateri, if you had to make it alone, can you see well enough to do it?"

Her throat suddenly tightened. She knew the dangers of such an escape, but it hadn't registered on her mind before this. He was saying that he and the Huron could be killed. She reached up and clutched the cross on her necklace. The feel of the twigs in her palm renewed her and she raised her head. "With God, all things are possible."

Looking at her steadily, he nodded and leaned back again. The wind rustled the feather on his headband against his shoulder, but he did not move.

"What is life like at the mission?"

He did not turn to her, but threw his head back. His long braids dangled down his back and scraped the round. "It is unlike anywhere in Iroquoia. We live as Christians, but also as Iroquois. Our tribes can't seem to understand that. Though we are Catholic and believe all that Jesus revealed of the Father, we are still as our ancestors bore us. We are both. And more."

"Yes. That's how I fell, but I can't make my uncle understand this either. Why does God not open their eyes?"

"Not everyone's eyes can be opened. Is it not so in the gospels? Even those who were there and saw Jesus make his miracles?"

"Yes. 'Blessed are they who have not seen, but believe.'"

His smile was genuine. "Doubting Thomas," he chuckled. "There are many in Iroquoia." His eyes moved over her for a time before he turned to the rippling river again. "And here you have such bad eyes and see quite clearly."

She nodded.

"What awakened you to Christ?" he asked.

She shook her head, uncertain. "I think I was always awake. I just did not understand what my heart knew."

He was silent for so long she wondered at it. His expression was one of curiosity but also of surprise and even something more. Was it awe? The steady concentration of his dark eyes suddenly made her shiver.

A wave splashed up the beach and he jumped up when the canoe came back into view. The Huron leapt of out of the boat and dragged it ashore. His leather stockings were soaked to his thighs. The Gandawague chief!" he panted, dragging the canoe up into the undergrowth. "He comes! Up the river!"

The Algonquin grabbed Kateri's arm and dragged her to her feet. She had only enough time to snatch her pouch from the ground before he pulled her into the forest. "You stay and watch," he called over his shoulder to the Huron. The shadows swallowed them as the Huron moved to another part of the shoreline, heading into the brush.

"What is happening?" she gasped. He continued to pull her. Her bare toes stubbed against tree roots and she bit her lip hard to keep from crying out when she tramped over the sharp spines of thistles.

"Your uncle is coming. Praise God he does not know us. Our friend will watch where he goes and tell us when all is well.

Farther into the darkening woods they went, scrambling over boulders and scampering uphill. Kateri's energy was spent but she wearily plodded on, even when the Algonquin mercilessly yanked on her arm. Finally, they came to a deer hollow and nestled into its hiding shadows. The Algonquin grew silent like a stone. Even his breathing was silent.

Kateri struggled to be quiet. Her lungs were bursting from exertion but she knew she must be as quiet as her companion.

The moments ticked by. A turkey call rattled the distant underbrush. Overhead, an eagle's cry echoed far over the thick wilderness. A crow mocked her from a pine tree but she did not look up at it. With fear tightening her throat, she considered the situation. *If Uncle catches us, how can it ever be explained? He will think I was being abducted.* Her companion still held her wrist and his proximity gave her courage, but her thoughts drifted toward the Huron, lying in wait for her uncle. The Huron had a musket and she knew her uncle had one too. "Will he fight my uncle?" she whispered.

He clutched her wrist tightly. "He is not trying to ambush him."

"But my uncle will try to kill him. What will your friend do?"

"He will defend himself."

Kateri leapt to her feet. "But he must not kill my uncle!"

He yanked her down again. "He will try not to…but he will do what he must to defend himself."

Kateri shut her eyes and clasped her hands together in prayer. *Oh Lord, my uncle is a proud man and he has done great things for his people. Please do not allow him to be hurt for my sake. I would rather die in his place. Oh merciful Jesus, hear my plea.*

A single musket shot rang out. Its report rolled up and down the mountainsides, echoing back in a thousand ghostly gunshots. Kateri let out a cry of alarm and clutched the Algonquin's arm.

He did not move, but concern was clearly visible in his eyes. "Stay here," he said, and rose. He pulled the grasses up around her and even gathered dried branches and brambles, covering her completely. "No matter what happens," he said quietly, "say nothing. Do nothing."

He moved away from her and, settling on a rock along the forest trail, he took his musket and powder horn from his shoulder, and set it beside him in easy reach. Next, he took up his tobacco pouch and casually filled his pipe. With flint and steel, he soon lit it, and eased back, puffing large round clouds of smoke.

In a matter of moments, the foliage parted and Kateri's uncle burst through, his musket in his hands. He glared at the Algonquin and cast a cursory glance around the clearing. "I am looking for two men and a woman. Have you seen them?"

The Algonquin dragged on the pipe and pursed his lips, blowing perfect smoke rings over his head. "I have seen no one and even less game. Little wonder when the likes of you go thrashing through the forest."

"They abducted my niece. I want her back."

The Algonquin yawned. "Well, as I said, I have seen no on for the last hour."

"Since you find no game anyway, I suppose you won't mind if I look about."

The Algonquin shrugged. "Suit yourself."

The chief used his musket to part the brush, thrashing brambles and ferns with its muzzle. He march up the trail and leapt atop a hollow log. From that vantage, he searched the immediate area and scowled when his eyes again fell on the Algonquin. "If you saw them but lied to me, I will kill you."

The Algonquin chuckled. "Strong words from a stranger. How do I know *you* did not abduct her yourself?"

With a curse under his breath, the chief jumped from the log and stood over the other. His nostrils flared. "Because I say so, and I am chief of the Turtle Clan of Gandawague. Who are you?"

"Just a hunter far from home. And I hope to make it back alive without confrontation. I have no quarrel with you. Unless..." He rose, musket in hand. "Unless you desire one."

The chief clenched his jaw. His eyes took in the clearing one last time before he tore back through the woods the way he came.

The Algonquin eased back to the boulder and smoked his pipe for at least another half hour before knocking its bowl against the side of the rock and emptying its dying cinders on the ground.

He tucked the pipe back into his pouch and moved into the brush, casting aside the branches and grasses that hid Kateri.

She was on her knees, lost in prayer. He gently tapped her shoulder and her eyes opened.

"Let us go."

They moved back down the trail to the river, but he made her wait in the shadows first while he stepped onto the rocky beach and greeted his friend the Huron with relief. "The shot. What was it?"

"I was pretending to shoot game. I hoped it would warn you that the chief was coming."

He smiled and rested his hand affectionately on the other's shoulder. "It did. It gave us just enough time to send him down the wrong trail again."

"He returned to the shore and got into his canoe and paddled back upstream. He was not happy."

The Algonquin made a sound of affirmation before turning to Kateri. "It's all clear. For now. But we dare not risk going to the settlement. We will have to push ahead and eat later. You may eat your own provisions."

"If you do not eat, I do not eat."

"Very well. Back into the canoe."

She climbed in and they shoved it into the water. Once they took their places in front and behind her, they set to rowing again. They did not stop until well after sundown.

Many days on the Mohawk passed and there was no further sign of their being followed. This made Kateri feel better but far from feeling entirely relieved.

Before long, the river's water became shallow. The Huron motioned for them to stop rowing and they beached the canoe under an elm. "There is no more river here. We must take this overland to the Hudson."

Kateri said nothing. She helped them turn the canoe over and tried to help them carry it, but she was shorter and they insisted she merely walk behind. She took their provisions from them and put the straps over her shoulders.

The two men traveled steadily, but Kateri soon tired and fell farther behind. The Huron noticed and motioned for his companion to lower the canoe. "We will rest for a while," said the Algonquin.

Kateri set down her burden. *Lord,* she prayed, *I am not angry at this illness that weakens me. After all, I became used to it long ago. But now it poses a danger to my companions who risk their life for me. If you could grant me the strength to go on I would not be such a burden to them.* Kateri listened to the gentle silence, wrapped in its peace and comfort. She felt God's presence surround her, felt his love, and though she was not bestowed more energy, the surging warmth in her shoulders told her that she was given something more intangible.

The Huron climbed a boulder and sat atop it. He scanned the treetops and the open meadow. Her cousin the Algonquin dropped down beside Kateri and pointed toward the wide blue sky. "You see the sky?" he asked.

She nodded, looking up but blinking away the bright sunshine.

"It is a circle. God created this great circle to show us the importance of circles. We sit in a circle at council. We dance in a circle at festivals. Even a drum is a circle. It is all circles. And life is a circle, too. We travel thinking we are going forward, but we usually end up at the place we started. Perhaps it was not our original journey. Perhaps we are finishing a journey started long before us."

Kateri watched his brown eyes gather reflections of clouds. His voice was like the breeze in its gentleness and calm. "Am I finishing a journey?"

Still staring at the sky, the Algonquin nodded. "It is our mother's journey. She took this same route from the Sault Mission to your father's village and now you are taking the same path back. It is all circles."

Kateri closed her eyes and absorbed his words. She tried to picture the vague image of her mother. "Circles," she whispered. *You had to make this journey first,* she said to the image, *so that I could make it home.* The thought changed her. She breathed in the sweet meadow grass and felt rejuvenated. "I am rested enough. Let's go on."

The Algonquin took the provisions from Kateri and allowed her to follow behind while they carried the canoe.

After a week they reached the wide Hudson River, and a week after that they finally reached the Lake of the Sacrament. A heavy mist rolled over the flat waters, and the sound of a loon echoed distantly. Kateri was encouraged during their long flight. Her uncle seemed to have given up his pursuit, and as the miles fell away, she felt the excitement of coming closer to her goal. But seeing this wide lake—that her Algonquin cousin said was one of many they must cross—weighed her heart with disquiet.

The canoe speared forward, gurgling gently over the somber waters. The mist ahead nestled on the lake, swallowing up what might lay beyond it. Kateri shivered under her rabbit cloak. The lake's gray murkiness seemed a foreboding omen, especially when all fell silent except for the lapping waves against the bark sides of the boat.

The canoe glided smoothly toward the shore and both companions seemed to search for something along the indistinct riverside. Beaching the craft, they motioned her to silence as they stepped onto shore. Each moved in his own direction, padding so softly over the river rocks that they made no sound. Soon each became like ghosts in the swallowing fog and disappeared completely.

Kateri sat motionless in the canoe. The time passed. There was no movement from the shore. Something splashed behind her and she turned to watch its wake ripple toward the canoe and spill onto the rocky beach with a hushed sound. She turned to the misty shoreline but could see nothing. How long was it since they left? It was difficult telling time in such fog. It was like one of her dreams, where reality slipped easily away.

Was this Purgatory, this constant waiting?

Kateri stretched her listening, trying to hear her companions, but still there was nothing.

"Kateri!"

It was only whisper but it still startled her and she threw her hand over her own mouth to keep from crying out. The Huron bent over her, looking at her curiously. "Come out of the canoe.

We have another."

She grabbed the provision sacks and followed him to a sand spit where two men were hauling a large canoe into the water. The stranger turned to her and smiled.

"Garonhiague!"

"I have been hiding this boat waiting for you. I am glad to see you are well, Kateri. The Lake of the Sacrament is only a small finger of the greater Lake Champlain. We still have many miles to go."

The boat was wider and more provisions covered by furs were stuffed in its ribs. The Huron helped Kateri in, and her heart was soothed by the men's easy confidence.

It took many more weeks to traverse the long Lake Champlain. They often stopped to trade more provisions or to trap game. The cottonwood leaves were slowly changing from green to yellow, and iciness nipped the air in the mornings and late evenings. Summer was giving way to autumn, and once they reached the Richelieu River it was evident the season had turned.

Kateri sat at the campfire, staring into its warm flames. The Oneida chief Garonhiague sat opposite her while the Algonquin sat beside her, rather protectively, she thought with a smile. The Huron was sharpening his knife. His face lay in shadows.

Garonhiague ducked his head to look at Kateri. "You have been smiling almost the whole journey."

Kateri shook her head. "I have not! I was worried for the first part, worried that my uncle would appear at any moment. But I put my trust in the Lord and he has brought me guardian angels to protect me and bring me safely to my new home."

Garonhiague looked from one companion to the other before throwing back his head in a loud laugh. The Huron raised his eyes but only blinked, but the Algonquin chuckled. "We are angels, my brothers," Garonhiague said, slapping his thighs. He shook his head. "We are not angels, little Kateri. But we are God's children. That is a fact." He settled down by the fire, stretching out on his back. He lit his pipe and puffed gently. The tobacco smoke rose in curls, joining the campfire's smoke in a mystical dance above their heads.

At last, after more weeks passed, the Richelieu joined the St. Lawrence River. To the west, the Portage River flowed into the St. Lawrence, creating Lake St. Paul.

Garonhiague pointed upward to mountains covered in spiring pine trees. Beyond that she could barely see another settlement. "That is Ville-Marie," he said. "Without their help, our little mission might not survive. And there, just on that island, is the Mission of St. Francis Xavier of Sault St. Louis, or as we like to call her, the Sault Mission."

Kateri raised the cross from her necklace and kissed it. Her heart filled with relief and prayers. They spilled over like the tears from her eyes.

The high stockade walls protected the chapel and residence. But Kateri noted with happiness the longhouses situated just outside the stockade walls. Here there was the familiar; hides stretched and drying on poles, ears of corn drying out on blankets, and smoke rising from longhouse roofs.

The women working near the longhouses noticed Kateri first, and they stopped their labors to observe her and her companions. Garonhiague raised his hand in greeting to many of them.

An older woman stood by her grinding stone. She let the empty cob fall from her fingers while trying to discern who Kateri was. Her dark hair streaked with gray was plaited into two long braids. The Algonquin approached her and gestured toward Kateri. "She is Kateri of the Turtle Clan. Kateri, this is Anastasia Tegonhatsihingo. She knew your mother."

"So long ago," said Anastasia. Her hand cupped Kateri's scarred face and she shook her head at the injuries. "There was sickness. She is dead, isn't she?"

"Yes. Long ago. I am her only surviving child. And I am finally Christian like her."

Anastasia put her arm around Kateri and led her into the village. "Share my longhouse. We are all we have now."

"I will share your longhouse, but you are wrong, Anastasia," said Kateri, her eyes glancing off one face only to light on another and another. "*This* is our family. I am happy to be here."

"You have come a long way. Rest. Eat."

"No. First I must go to the priests and be blessed."

She left Anastasia's arms and walked through the stockade's open gate. The chapel was empty, but she was drawn to the crucifix at the altar and she knelt there to offer thanks. She stayed so long that her companions came in search of her, bringing three priests.

Kateri rose and bowed her head before them. "Father, bless me."

The tallest priest stepped forward to do so, laying his hand on her head. Kateri sighed, feeling the strength of the Holy Spirit fill her before she raised her eyes. "I have a letter."

She pulled it forth and handed it to the priest. He tore the seal and read before searching Kateri's face.

"What is it, Father Jacques?" asked the shorter priest.

"It is from Father de Lamberville. He writes, 'This is Kateri Tekakwitha. I baptized her this Easter and I have no doubt that by the time she reaches you, she will be well prepared to receive Holy Eucharist. She is unlike any other Mohawks whom we have seen before. I am sorry to lose her, but her life was in danger if she stayed, though she offered to stay. Most Reverend Father, I send you this treasure. Guard it well.'"

He looked up from the paper to examine Kateri anew, from her disheveled hair to her bare and bloody feet. "A treasure," he said without conviction. "We must see *this* for ourselves."

CHAPTER SEVEN

Life at the Sault Mission was different from Gandawague. Before the sun rose, bells would call them all to prayer. Two Masses were celebrated and Kateri gladly attended both, though only one was required. After Mass, the Iroquois recited a rosary, contemplating the life of Jesus through the eyes of his mother, Mary. The evening prayers called Vespers were sung in the late afternoon, concluding with the Benediction of the Blessed Sacrament.

Kateri did not yet receive Holy Communion, and she longed for it. This was the actual body of Christ on earth, and it was her greatest desire to partake of it. This was the same bread Jesus himself blessed, broke, and shared with his apostles, the same bread he said would give eternal life. Without it, her baptism was only half-fulfilled.

Yet the priests did not offer it to her. "Patience," she told herself. "God's time is not Man's time. There is always something to be gained from learning patience."

Though she did not yet know them well, she delighted in the three priests that served the mission. First, there was Father Jacques Fremin who seemed to be in charge of the others. Then there was Father Pierre Cholenec, who was very short in stature, and finally Father Claude Chauchetière, the oldest of the three.

Kateri continued her chores, walking from the Iroquois settlement outside the mission walls to within the mission precincts. There, many white families lived. The only white Kateri had seen before were priests and trappers. She now saw women and children and was pleased to see that she shared much in common with these strangers.

Kateri trudged across the mission square carrying a heavy bundle of corncobs in a blanket. A white child, a girl, sat in the middle of the square crying and cradling something. It was only when Kateri was nearly beside her that she recognized the ragdoll in the girl's hands, but one of the arms was missing. She slid the heavy burden to the ground and bent over, brushing the little girl's hair aside. "Why do you weep? Is it for your doll?"

The little white girl looked up at Kateri with wet eyes. She did not understand Mohawk and Kateri spoke no French, but she seemed to know by Kateri's gentle tone that no harm was meant. The child lifted the doll and showed her the damage. The material was torn, with loose threads dangling down. Kateri smiled. She reached into her bundle and withdrew a dried cob. She took the old silk from the ear and peeled off the layers of dry husk and began to fold.

Soon, she constructed a little doll from the husks with the silk tucked in the top for hair before a shadow drew over them both.

The child's mother swooped down and caught the child up in her arms. She spoke harshly to Kateri in French though Kateri could well understand the tone.

The little girl waved to Kateri over her mother's shoulder and Kateri waved back.

"The whites do not understand our customs," said Kateri's cousin as she approached from behind. This was her mother's cousin with whom she lived along with Anastasia, but Kateri could not see anything of her mother in the woman's often mistrustful eyes.

"Do you know what she said?"

Her cousin made a huffing noise. "It is best you don't know."

Kateri lifted her burden again. "Most of the white women here are not like that. They are kind to me."

"Because you are new. You will see. They will treat you like the rest of us."

"But we are all Christian here. Surely it does not matter. 'There is neither Jew nor Greek, there is neither slave nor free, there is male and female; for you are all one in Christ Jesus.'"

"You will see. It matters to them."

Kateri watched the mother and child finally disappear into their cabin. "Then I will pray on it."

Kateri did not seem to notice any difference in treatment when she met the white families in the chapel for Mass. Many seemed to make kind remarks to her in French, which she acknowledged with a nod.

"They speak kindly to you because of how you pray," whispered Anastasia before the Mass one day.

"How I pray?"

"Why yes. So you do not know? Your prayer is different from the rest."

Kateri's heart warmed from worry. She frowned. "Am I doing something wrong?"

Anastasia chuckled and pressed Kateri's arm. "You? Do something wrong? I do not think it is possible!" Her laughter died, and she stared Kateri in the eyed. "You do not know, do you?"

"Anastasia, please tell me."

"Kateri..." Her voice softened, sounding something like the rush of wind echoing off Lake St. Paul. "When *you* pray," she said slowly, "the world seems to stop for you. The Holy Spirit himself encompasses you, surely. You...*become* prayer."

Kateri considered and finally shook her head. "But that is only because I love to be in God's presence. He welcomes me. He welcomes everyone."

Anastasia chuckled low in her throat. "Not like he welcomes you," she said under her breath.

They walked to the chapel and when Mass ended, they sat quietly after the last prayer of the rosary was said. They stayed for a long time before Anastasia tapped Kateri's arm and the two finally left the chapel. Anastasia looked up into the wintry sky and hugged her arms and stepped aside for the water drops cascading down from the icicles in the surrounding pine trees. "Come sit with me inside by the fire, Kateri," said the older woman.

Kateri followed silently. She was still suspended in the warmth of their prayers and did not notice the cold. She sat obediently beside Anastasia, who broke several twigs and cast them into the little fire in their corner of the longhouse.

Kateri watched the flames. The flickering light glittered in her eyes and its mesmerizing amber drew her into a dream state. Soon the flames seemed to fall away and she saw Jesus standing on a mountaintop. His clothes were a brilliant white and he was looking at her. Gently he raised his arms, beckoning. Her dream body obeyed, and climbed the mountain. Vaguely, she was aware that she did not tire while climbing, nor was her breath short from the exertion. Her feet, though still bare, were clean and free of scratches and bruises, and her skin—as in another vision—seemed to take on an unnatural glow. The closer she got to him, her joy grew, filling her heart with its burning fullness. Only a few paces away, she reached forward, expecting to feel his hands on hers.

"Kateri! Do you hear me?"

The pulse of life rushed back into her. The warmth of Jesus fell away replaced by the cold of winter. Her skin flushed not with glowing health, but with its accustomed weakness, and she seemed to shrink while sitting before the fire, aware again of her surroundings and that Anastasia was talking to her.

"Yes, Anastasia. What were you saying?"

"I was telling you of the lives of the saints. The Catholic saints are very much like our ancestors whom we have cherished. And in a way, they *are* our ancestors, for we are all the children of God whether white or Mohawk."

"I like to listen to their stories, Anastasia. I like to know how they lived their life in God. They are good examples to us, even though many lived long ago."

"Devotion to God does not change with the times. Devotion is devotion."

Kateri smiled. "You are right, as always, Anastasia."

"They lived lives of penance, sacrificing their health and their livelihood to the great glory of God. It is a difficult choice. As an old woman, I find some sacrifices too hard."

"Sacrifice." Kateri watched the flames, feeling the echo of her vision at the edge of her senses. "I have not yet been able to touch Jesus because I do not give enough."

"What did you say, my dear? What have you not given?"

"More in sacrifice. 'Much will be required of the person entrusted with much, and still more will be demanded of the person entrusted with more.'"

Anastasia glanced at Kateri's scarred feet, now blotched from cold. "You give much already."

Kateri's mind was still on Jesus who remained unreachable in her visions. "I need only a small amount of food. I will have one meal a day instead of three. I will fill my hunger with prayer instead. Excuse me, Anastasia, while I go to speak with the Lord."

"Wait, Kateri."

But she already rose and pushed aside the heavy hide hanging in front of the longhouse entrance. She walked over the cold ground on her bare feet and escaped into the woods. She breathed a sigh of relief as she entered its stillness. Though it was good to belong to a Christian community at last and go to chapel with the others, her consolation still lay in the solitude of the woodlands. Without the noise and chatter of others, her heart could be opened to the wonders of God, and her soul filled with his presence.

When the Angelus bells rang at noon, Kateri recited that prayer at her place under the trees. Though the air was heavy with frost, she did not feel the chill, and it surprised her to look up after her prayers to find Father Cholenec standing above her.

He smiled. Its kindly intention reminded her of a grandfather's smile, though he was not nearly old enough to be one. His shoulder-length brown hair blew in the breeze and tangled on his collar. "Forgive me for interrupting, Kateri. But I've been looking for you."

Kateri rose. It was her custom to keep her face lowered slightly to protect her eyes. "Yes, Father?"

"I have been observing you, child, and I have noted your piety. There is a difference between you and the others. Not that the others are less devoted in their faith, but in you...well...there is *more.*"

Kateri waited for him to continue. She did not feel flattered by his words. After all, they were simply the truth and she could not take credit for mere truth.

Father Cholenec struggled for words. Kateri wished to help him and raised her face and squinted. "What is it you wish to tell me, Father?"

"I wish to tell you it was decided amongst my fellow priests that you will received communion at Christmas."

Kateri's heart pounded with joy, but she only lowered her face.

"I know it is unusual for someone new to the mission to receive Holy Communion so early upon their arrival," the priest went on, "but you are a special case. You seem in communion with God and the spiritual life like none other I have seen before. I see no reason to delay your communication. But I warn you. When others hear of it, they will become jealous, for many of them have been here a long time and still have not received the Lord's body."

"Why?"

"Though it is true the laity do not receive communion but once a year, it is a special sacrament and must be reserved for those in a state of grace."

"Do you believe I am in a state of grace?"

"Kateri, I do not think there has been a moment of my knowing you that you have *not* been in a state of grace."

She nodded. "I am pleased and grateful for this gift, Father. Now more than ever, I am anxious for Christmas."

Even though she practiced patience, Advent moved slowly and Christmas took its time arriving. Once it had, Kateri tried to keep her excitement in check. She alone would receive Holy Communion and she knew what a precious gift it was. Both white and Iroquois decorated the chapel for Christmas with greenery and candles. Kateri recalled the last Christmas at Gandawague and how she had come closer to understanding Christ at the wondrous celebration of music and light.

She knelt at her place in the chapel and closed her eyes to welcome the presence of God. '*O, Lord Jesus Christ, Son of the living God, who by the will of the Father and with the cooperation of the Holy Spirit have by your death given life to the world: deliver me by this, your most sacred body and blood, from all my sins and from every evil. Make me always cling to your commandments and never permit me to be separated from you. Amen.*'

The mass began and when the time came for Kateri to receive the Host, she felt as if she were floating toward the altar. When she kneeled and took the bread into her mouth, she felt the world fall away as it often did in her dream state. But this time, she had within her very being the Body of God and she savored every last morsel.

Afterward, many of the people nodded to her politely but still others gave her a wide berth, puzzlement on their faces, and fear, too. "Anastasia," she whispered, "Why do they look at me oddly? Did I do something wrong?"

"My dear," she said, her husky voice rasping in Kateri's ear. "Don't you know? You changed. You glowed with the light of Christ. We have never seen anything like this."

"Do you mean that what I felt inside was somehow visible to all?"

"Only those nearest. But yes. I think God has marked you."

Kateri's heart pounded. "What do you mean, Anastasia?"

The older woman smiled. The light of the Mass candles still seemed to glitter in her bright eyes. "I am a lover of the lives of the saints. I have heard too many stories not to know one when I see one." She chuckled and pressed Kateri's hand before trudging back toward the longhouse.

Kateri watched her go with a strange sensation tickling up her spine. "I am not afraid to be a saint, my God," she said to the quiet night. "I am afraid I will never be worthy of it."

As the weeks wore on and winter drew its frosty mantle over the hills and trees, Kateri felt the weight of that long ago sickness bear down on her. Each day became a trial to complete her tasks. Without anyone's notice, she stopped often to rest.

Yet Father Cholenec *did* notice.

Kateri was preparing a travois, filling it with what the hunters would need for the winter hunt. Many of the Iroquois would go, including the women, but Kateri planned on staying behind. The effort to pack the travois was almost too much and she sat beside it, catching her breath.

"Kateri," said Father Cholenec.

She stood quickly and began to pack again. "Father," she acknowledged, without looking up.

Gently, he took her hand and looked at it. "You are very pale. I think you need to rest a moment."

"I am fine, Father. I am only a little fatigued."

"Anastasia tells me you are not going on the hunt. This is very serious. I understand that the winter hunt is a very important part of Mohawk life."

"That is true. But I feel I am too weak and would be a burden to them."

"I do not see that. I see an opportunity for you to be close with your people. This is just as important as your silent prayer in the woods. After all, we are the Body of Christ and as such, we are a community of believers. We work in community, live in community, and worship in community. Even God himself is a community of the Trinity. Surely you cannot deny that?"

"No, but..."

"These are important moments for us. You are still a young woman and a young woman needs to participate in these things. I insist you go on the hunt It will do you good. The camps will not be any more difficult than your chores here."

Kateri sighed, glancing at the priest's crucifix hanging over his black wool robe. "I will do as you say, Father."

After several weeks, Kateri saw the wisdom in the priest's insistence. Though fatigued, she was happy to hear the old songs of the hunt mixed with Christian hymns and to hear the exaggerated hunting stories around the night fires. Yet even in the company of people she understood with old and new customs, Kateri felt distant from the others and often made her way alone into the wilderness to find the only peace she knew.

The bark gave way under the knife blade. The cross was soon etched on the bark, and Kateri knelt in the snow before it. She was very much aware that the whites at the mission treated her with special care, but the Iroquois, too, seemed to hold her in esteem. "I have never desired such attention, Lord. Why is it given to me now?"

She noticed her cousin's friend the Huron always seemed to be close by. Was he observing her, or was it mere coincidence? Looking back through the straight stands of birch, she saw smoke rising from the fires. The winter sun hung low along the horizon, just skimming the tops of the naked trees. Now it was shining golden near the ridge of the distant hills and would soon set. It was time to return to the camp to see what successes the hunt brought. And once the stories were told and the deer dressed, slowly the hunters would return to their lodges to sleep.

Kateri nestled by her fire, watching the coals turn to glowing embers. Not all the hunters had returned, but the work was exhausting and many settled quickly under their furs to sleep.

At dawn Kateri was startled from sleep. A woman was bending over her, shrieking and shaking her fists. At first, Kateri could not understand her words, but slowly she focused and widened her eyes in disbelief.

"So!" the woman cried. Her shrill voice awakened the others, who slowly rose from their mats and furs. "The weakling shows her true self! You would steal my husband because you have none of your own!"

CHAPTER EIGHT

Everyone was shouting at once. Kateri merely sat, staring at the cold fire ring. The man beside her rose to his feet and tried to speak, but no one would allow him. Finally, he cast an apologetic glance to Kateri before throwing up his hands and exiting the lodge. Some of the men followed him but many of the women stayed, listening to the woman, Smiling One, harangue Kateri.

"These others talk about how pious you are," went on Smiling One, "but I see you for what you are."

"Hush, Smiling One," cautioned another woman, Anna. She was the same age as Smiling One, but there were gray hairs streaking her braids. "You must be wrong. Everyone knows Kateri is not like the others."

"She has fooled you too, then. I want to know why she was trying to steal my husband."

Kateri still sat on her furs, her eyes downcast. She said nothing for there was nothing to say. She did not understand what was happening and knew that Truth would vindicate her.

"Kateri," said Anna, bending down to touch her shoulder. "Tell us what happened."

The women gathered closer, ringing her. Smiling One stood

with her arms crossed tightly over her chest, her expression belying her name.

Kateri shook her head. "There is nothing to say."

Anna stood back and looked at the others. Smiling One nodded vigorously. "This is not the first time I have seen her with my husband. I tried to dismiss it as mere jealousy, but I saw them talking quietly before. She often goes away by herself. What is she doing if not some mischief?"

Kateri refused to reply and, one by one, the women walked away leaving only Smiling One, who nodded with self-satisfaction before she turned her heel.

I have no fear of them, she said to the Lord, *for you are with me and you are Truth and Light. Whom shall I fear?*

Smiling One said no more words on the matter, but she made it clear by her actions and manner that it was not over between them. She whispered to the others when Kateri came near and she offered remarks about her character at the campfires, just loud enough to be heard by everyone else.

By the time they all returned to the Sault Mission, many others had joined in the rumors about Kateri. At last it was brought to the attention of Father Cholenec.

Kateri had just sat exhausted by the cold fire ring in her longhouse when a young boy flung back the hide covering the door. "Kateri, Father Cholenec is calling for you. It is about what happened at the hunt."

Kateri sighed with weariness as she slowly rose. "I suppose this must be done," she said, following him.

Father Cholenec sat on a carved chair in his cabin, mulling over papers before him. The candle on his desk flickered as she entered but he did not look up immediately. His eyes were concentrated on his work, and she watched his brown eyes dart from one line of text to another, following the small black characters that made up the white man's writing.

At last he looked up, and his expression changed from

concentrated indifference to sudden concern. He straightened and rested his hands on the desk, enclosing his fingers together. "Kateri, I was disturbed by unusual reports from the hunting expedition."

Kateri raised her head and squinted at the priest's face, but she said nothing.

He watched her face for a time before he rose and slowly paced around his desk. "A woman named Smiling One made some accusations." He glanced at her but still she made no reply. He shook his head. "I do not know you well, Kateri. I only know what I see and what I hear. What I hear…is atrocious. But what I see does not conform to what I hear. You must explain it to me."

"I cannot explain what I do not know I am being accused of."

Exasperated, Father Cholenec sighed. "Smiling One accuses you of immoral behavior with her husband. She claims she found him lying beside you one morning."

"She did find him there. That is undeniable."

"Do not be coy with me. This is a serious charge. This sort of behavior will not be tolerated at the mission. Anyone found to be of low moral character will be asked to leave."

Kateri blinked slowly. *Lord my Savior, comfort me!* "I am not guilty of what she accuses me."

Father Cholenec seemed to ease with relief. "That may be your tale," he said, squaring his shoulders again. "But Smiling One and her husband are here to settle the matter."

Behind her, Kateri felt a breeze as the door opened and Smiling One and her husband entered. They bowed to the priest. "Now tell me," Father Cholenec said to them. "What happened?"

Smiling One launched into a long speech, ending with her catching Kateri with her husband. The husband stood silently and once or twice rolled his eyes.

Father Cholenec looked to the husband and asked him to explain.

"As I tried to say before," he said, glancing angrily at his wife,

"I was exhausted after the hunt. Kateri's sleeping area looked to be empty. Father, to be truthful, I did not care whether it was empty or not. It was closest to the door and I was dead on my feet. I did not desire to grope my way through the dark to find my wife. I simply stopped as the closest, warmest fur and fell into an immediate deep sleep. That is *all*."

Father Cholenec repressed a smile as he turned his back on them all. "Is that what you say, Kateri?"

"If he says it, it must be true. I do not know. I was asleep at the time."

Smiling One bristled. "You do not believe them, do you?"

"I think that your imagination...and perhaps jealousy...has clouded your judgment, Smiling One. I believe we have just heard the truth."

Kateri breathed and praised God.

Smiling One said nothing and stalked out of the room, leaving her husband to give an apologetic shrug before he followed her out.

The season passed into spring, and one day an Oneida woman came to the Sault Mission.

Kateri was at the gate when the woman passed through. Her step was uncertain, and her demeanor was fearful, so Kateri stopped her chores and met her there.

"I am Kateri. And I welcome you to the Mission of St. Francis Xavier of Sault St. Louis."

"Then I am in the right place," she said, lowering her bundle to the ground. "I have traveled a long way to come here."

"Are you Christian?"

"Yes. But I was not a very good one until recently. My name is Marie Thérèse Tegaiaguenta."

"Come inside. I will get you water." Kateri pulled the woman's arm and brought her to the square. Marie Thérèse sat while Kateri scooped water from a bucket into a gourd dipper and handed it to her. The woman drank and wiped her mouth before setting the gourd aside. She looked at Kateri's scarred face and nodded. "You have seen much pain, too."

"Yes," she said smiling. "But that was long ago. Now I have joy because I can live the life of a Christian."

"That is what I am seeking. Two years ago, we went on our winter hunt. But almost immediately things began to go wrong. Weapons were lost when a travois broke, and a blizzard lasted for weeks. Many died of the cold, and some that survived killed others so that their chances of survival would be better. It was horrible. And when I thought it could get no worse, my husband died. I made a promise to God that if he should allow me to survive that ordeal, I would seek him out and truly be his servant. As you can see, here I am, and I have been working hard to be God's handmaid. It is not always easy."

"That is true. But you found in your suffering a way to heal through God. That is the best path. You chose well."

A smile brightened Marie Thérèse's face. "I have found the right mission and the right soul, it seems."

Kateri put her arm around the woman's shoulders and led her into the compound. "There is a great fellowship among the Iroquois of the mission," she said to Marie Thérèse. "But for me, I like to go to the woods and be alone with God."

Marie Thérèse waked silently with Kateri, looking down at her feet. "I notice you wear no moccasins. Why?"

Kateri lifted her head to catch a breeze off the lake. It lifted the loose hairs dangling in her eyes. "It reminds me of the suffering of my Lord. I wear no moccasins and I eat only one meal a day."

Marie Thérèse stopped and gazed into Kateri's face with dark wide eyes. "God has blessed me. He has given you to me to guide me. This is what I seek."

"Let us seek it together."

Kateri took her arm again and walked with her to the longhouse.

She introduced Marie Thérèse to Anastasia and to those of the Confraternity of the Holy Family, which was made up of the older members of the compound. Marie Thérèse met them with respectful bows. Once she and Kateri left the longhouse, she whispered, "You belong to the Confraternity? Only the old ones are invited."

"Nevertheless. They invited me on Palm Sunday. It is a great honor. They are very holy people." Kateri ignored Marie Thérèse's acclamations and led her across the muddy square to the chapel. But before they reached it, Marie Thérèse said, "Kateri, there is someone at the gate waving at you."

Kateri squinted but it did no good. "Who is it? I cannot see."

"It looks like a trapper. A Frenchman."

Kateri excused herself, bidding the woman to go inside without her, and started for the gate, but with a moment of hesitation, Marie Thérèse scurried after her.

The trapper doffed his fur hat when Kateri neared. "*Demoiselle* Kateri," he said, squeezing the hat between his large fingers.

"George," she said with a smile. She touched his hand. "It has been a long time."

"The winter was harsh for all of us. The trapping has not been good. I ask that you pray for me."

"I will. I always do."

"My wife, too, is ill. If the trapping is better, then I can go home to her."

"Then my prayers will be all the more fervent for you and your success." She touched his hand again. "Don't worry. All of Heaven will be praying for you."

He smiled a gap-toothed grin and lifted her hand to kiss. "*Merci, demoiselle.* I know that God answers your prayers. Here." He took an otter skin from a bag strapped over his shoulder, but Kateri shook her head.

"I cannot take this. You need it."

"No, no, you take it."

"I have no need of it."

"Surely it can be used for someone here. Maybe this good friend of yours," and he gesture toward Marie Thérèse.

Kateri nodded. "Your gift *will* be used by someone here. Be assured of that. And now I must go to the chapel in order to ask God to help you."

"*Merci, demoiselle.*" He bowed and backed away from the gate, before untying his horse and mounting. "*Adieu!*"

Marie Thérèse watched him ride away before tuning a puzzled expression toward Kateri. "Even the white trappers know you?"

Kateri was already walking back toward the chapel and stopped to consider her companion's question. At last she shrugged. "I allow myself to be known to them. Some of the Iroquois feel we are different from the whites and must not associate with them. I do not think we are different."

"We are treated differently."

"You sound like my cousin. We are all God's children. When we start thinking as God thinks and not as Man, then we truly will be God's children." She walked a few paces before turning again. "Come along to the chapel."

Father Cholenec was there, lighting candles, and she introduced him to Marie Thérèse.

"You are welcomed to our mission. Stay close to this one," he said in a loud whisper and pointing to Kateri. "She will lead you on the righteous path."

Marie Thérèse nodded, seemingly too stunned to speak.

"Kateri, I have been looking for you."

Kateri had just lowered to her knees when she turned to the priest. "Yes, Father?"

"I have a special task for you. I have a message I wish for you to take to the hospital in Ville-Marie."

"Ville-Marie? Are you certain you wish for *me* to go?"

"It is not far. The journey will do you good. I think you will be surprised by Ville-Marie."

Kateri had heard from the others how big a village Ville-Marie was. Some of the Iroquois who went returned with fantastic stories of the numbers of whites there and of the marvelous sights and buildings. Such things never attracted Kateri but she was as curious as any other.

But a journey on her own across the lake and into the hills? Since her coming to the mission, she had not traveled far from its walls.

"Very well, Father. If you desire it, then I will go."

CHAPTER NINE

Kateri did not go alone. The priest insisted the Huron accompany her and he gladly accepted.

When they arrived in Ville-Marie, she was stunned by its size. Their longhouses were not only bigger, but also peaked, wider, and made of wood and stone. Some of the streets were paved in bricks, and tall cressets lit the streets when night fell.

Kateri stepped into the street and was nearly run down by a horse-drawn carriage. The Huron yanked her back out of the way, and they both watched the strange vehicle turn a corner and disappear. "I did not know such places and things existed," she gasped aloud.

The Huron nodded. "I have been to big cities before. Ville-Marie is not different, except it is a French city."

"And you speak this language, my brother?"

"Yes. I was taught French long ago by a Blackrobe."

Kateri stayed close to the tall Huron, and gawked at the unusual clothing of the richer women and men. The fabrics were not made of skins, but fine woven cloth.

"Kateri, come this way. I wish to show you something."

Kateri's weak eyes filled with the many sights of Ville-Marie, but once they turned the corner, her eyes widened. Down a long tree-lined avenue, past a green pasture, was a building, one much taller than the others. Its walls were made of stone and a stone tower spired heavenward. At its peak stood a cross.

"Is this their chapel?" she whispered, craning her neck to look at its full height.

"It is a church. We can look inside for a moment."

They climbed the stairs together and once they reached huge wooden doors, they peered inside. She looked down the long, dark nave which arched high to its wood beam ceiling. Coronas holding rings of candles hung from the heights. At the end of the nave, shining golden behind a carved screen, was the sanctuary and the tabernacle holding the consecrated hosts. Kateri froze. The Beauty of it all made it difficult to breathe. She took a step forward to approach the tabernacle and the huge crucifix that hung above it, but the Huron snatched at her cloak and dragged her back.

"You must not." His eyes darted to the robed figures milling near the screen that separated the nave from the sanctuary. "We are not allowed."

"Why not? We are Catholic. This is our church."

He took a deep breath and exhaled it through his nose. The sparse light shadowed his eyes. "Because we are Indians and they are white. This is their church."

"But—"

"Kateri. I know what should be, but it is not so. Let us leave now before we are asked to."

The Huron was already heading for the door. Kateri looked back regrettably to the sanctuary. "There will be a day soon when I will walk in your golden light," she said to the distant crucifix. She genuflected to the tabernacle before following the Huron outside.

"I must deliver this message to the hospital," she said to him when they reached the bottom step and entered the sunshine. She felt the package in her pouch, felt its weight, and wondered again what the wonderful writing said.

"It is this way," he said gesturing. They continued down the main street and came to a great iron gate decorated with metal vines and crosses. They rang the bell and waited. A woman all in black and white appeared. Upon her breast hung a crucifix.

"Is this a mission?" Kateri asked.

The Huron shook his head. "This is a convent. The woman is a nun. We call her 'Sister'."

"A nun. What is that?"

But the nun cut her question short, reaching the gate, yet she did not open it. "Yes?" she asked through the bars.

Kateri marveled at her starched white collar, the velvety dark robes, and the crucifix, the body of Christ rendered in some smooth white material, and the black wood of the cross with brass fittings.

The Huron bowed to her. "Sister," he said in French, "we are from the Sault Mission and we have a letter from Father Cholenec."

"I see. You are welcome, then." Out of her robes she removed a ring of keys. She chose one, inserted it into the gate, and pulled it open. "Come," she said with a tilt to her head. They followed her to the end of a garden path and up a flight of stairs to a door. She took out another key and unlocked that, and opened it. She waited for Kateri and the Huron to walk through before she locked it behind them. They stood under the shade of a long arcade that stretched around the perimeter of the building. In the center was a garden and in the center of that stood a statue of the Virgin Mary.

The nun looked at Kateri. "I will take your letter."

Kateri pulled the package from her pouch and handed it to the nun.

The nun looked at it and nodded. "Wait here." She turned and seemed to glide down the arcade, disappearing through door. Across the cloister, Kateri saw more nuns tending to the little garden around the Virgin's statue. Some were scrubbing the floor of the arcade ahead of them.

The Huron raised his chin, and stared at the rooftop.

"What place is this?" asked Kateri.

"This is a convent and a hospital. The convent is a place where holy women come to live to devote their lives to Christ."

Kateri listened to the silence. "Where are their children?"

"They have none. They never marry. They devote their lives to God instead of having husbands and children."

Intrigued, Kateri watched them work together, her mind racing. "I did not know such places existed," she said quietly.

The Huron sighed again.

The nun returned with a package. "These are the herbs and medicines your priest requested. Make certain you take it straight back to them."

"Thank you," said the Huron with a bow. He handed the package to Kateri. The nun watched her put it carefully in her sack.

"Straight back," she said again before leading them to the gate and repeating the ritual of the keys.

Once the gate whined shut, Kateri wrapped her fingers around the bars and rested her cheek against the cold iron. "A convent. I like this Ville-Marie, Brother. It has opened my eyes just as Father Cholenec said it would."

Two days later they returned to the mission. It was exhausting travel for Kateri, but she could not contain her excitement when she saw Marie Thérèse again.

"Such things I saw!" she said, as they settled with her female cousin and Anastasia by their hearth fire. "The church is so tall and beautiful. Heaven must be like that. I could smell the scent of incense still lingering in the air. The greatest thing of all was the convent. Did you know that spiritual women could devote themselves entirely to God? They do not marry nor have children. They work and live together and pray to God all day. What a marvelous gift!"

"Gift to whom?" her cousin asked. "Without children, there are no more people at all. A woman must marry and have children. It is time you sought a husband, Kateri."

She lowered her face. It was that same argument again. Even among Christians!

"Your cousin in right," said Anastasia. "I am too old and so is she." She elbowed Kateri's cousin playfully. "You must bring children into the world."

Her cousin patted her hand. "Your children can be disciples."

Anastasia leaned forward and spoke in low tones, though all who gathered could hear her. "The Huron has asked for you."

"My friend and brother?" Kateri's heart sank. Perhaps that was why he followed her on the hunt, keeping watch of her, and volunteered to take her to Ville-Marie. She did not want to disappoint him, but her mind had been made up on the matter long ago. "You must tell him for me that I decided years ago to never marry. Now I see why. It has been to become a nun."

The others fell silent. But Marie Thérèse's eyes shined with dreams. Kateri took her hands and nodded excitedly. "Yes. I had hoped you, too, would cherish this idea and we can become sisters in Christ together.

"Yes, Kateri. It is a marvelous idea. Let us go to the priest now."

Marie Thérèse helped Kateri to her feet.

Father Cholenec was not in, but the tall Father Fremin greeted Kateri, thanking her again for her journey.

"I am grateful to have been sent, Father, for I have seen what God has surely desired me to see. I saw the convent there, saw the holy sisters living in their sacred communion. Father, Marie Thérèse and I wish also to become nuns."

Father Fremin said nothing for a long time. At first, Kateri wondered if he heard her, until he took a breath, opened his mouth, and laughed.

The sound of it was like blows to her body. She shrunk at each new guffaw, lowering her face. Marie Thérèse clutched Kateri's arm.

"Surely you are not serious," he said at last, chuckling. "Indians do not become nuns."

"Why not?"

Father Fremin composed his features into an indulgent smile, much as a parent would give to a silly child. "You are such simple people. Of course being as close to the earth as you are, you are keenly aware of God. But becoming *religieuse* needs the intelligence and comportment you Iroquois do not possess. It is a sweet thought you have in this, Kateri, but it is not proper to continue with such dreams. You will only be disappointed. Content yourself with going to chapel and living here at the mission."

Kateri stared at her bare feet a long time. They had become hard with callouses and all the scars had grown over with layers of new scars. She had accepted many sufferings throughout her life. First, it was the loss of her family and the disfigurement of her face and eyes. Then it was the persecution by her own family and people because of her strong belief in God. But now, the greatest hurt of all came from a man who should have understood her best. She could not believe that her cousin had been right about the whites and that the Huron's fears in Ville-Marie were justified.

She felt Marie Thérèse squeezed her arm again. Clearly, she was waiting for Kateri to defend their position. Kateri raised her head at last and glanced once at Marie Thérèse, hoping she would comprehend.

"Yes, Father. I understand. Come, Marie Thérèse."

Marie Thérèse kept he silence until they were outside. "Why did you say nothing? He insulted us. Called us children!"

Kateri nodded, squinting into the sunlight. "That is how he sees us. I did not listen when my cousin or the Huron tried to tell me this. Now I see for myself. It is God's pleasure that it be more difficult for us, Marie Thérèse. We will make our own vows of virginity and poverty. We will live this life of penance without benefit of a convent. And we will still serve the Lord."

"But how can we—"

"In God, all things are possible. We serve not for ourselves or even for our own generation. But like the Israelites wandering in the desert, they suffered for the generations that came after. One day, our people will go to the great church in Ville-Marie and our women will become nuns in convents. Just not today."

"How can you be so certain of yourself?"

Kateri stopped and gazed upward. Even the sky seemed blurry today, yet she felt as if she were part of the sky, in it, looking down. "I don't know. I just know that it will be. Oh, Marie Thérèse. I feel so weak suddenly." The words barely left her lips before she collapsed into her friend's arms.

CHAPTER TEN

Shards of light filtered in through her fluttering lids, and Kateri cringed at the brightness. She felt the furs beneath her and slowly came to realize she was on her own pallet. She longed to raise her hand to her face but it felt too heavy to lift.

"Try to relax," said the soothing voice of Marie Thérèse. Beside her was the blurry figure she knew to be Anastasia.

Her lips felt dry when they parted and she spoke in only harsh whispers. "How long?"

"Two days," said Marie Thérèse. "You are very weak. Don't try to speak."

"I will soon be with my Lord," she whispered. Her limbs felt as if they were afire, and she gasped suddenly with the pain.

"What can you do for her?" cried Anastasia.

Marie Thérèse jumped up and ran from the longhouse. She wasn't gone long before she returned with Father Cholenec. He knelt beside her pallet and lifted her hand. "Look what I have brought you, Kateri. See. They are pictures of saints. I know how you like to hear the stories of the saints. You can look at their faces and know that they suffered even as you suffer. But they are now in the divine presence where all suffering is gone. Look at their faces, Kateri, and know your hope is in their eyes."

For days after, Kateri could not move because of the pain. When she could, she lifted a saint card close to her eyes and looked at their carefully drawn faces. "Tell me of my patron, Saint Katherine," she would ask of the woman sitting with her, and they would recount the tale until they could speak no more. Kateri never tired of hearing the stories, and she listened to one after another, all the while looking at the prayer cards and at their mysterious faces.

"You see," she said to Marie Thérèse "We have our little convent now. I am doing penance for all of you. But tell Anastasia that she must be careful chopping wood. I am afraid she does not see the stump behind her."

Marie Thérèse leaned closer. "Kateri. What are you saying? How do you know what Anastasia is doing?"

Kateri smiled and gazed with blurry blankness up into the longhouse ceiling. "But I can see her. Tell her to be careful."

Marie Thérèse looked at Smiling One and without a word, told her to sit with Kateri while she went outside. Walking to the woodpile, she saw no one, but then she went to the cooking fire and saw Anastasia chopping kindling. Behind her was a stump and she was backing slowly toward it. Marie Thérèse cried out, and Anastasia stopped, stumbling a little over the edge of the stump. She looked behind and pressed her hand to her heart.

"Marie Thérèse, if you had not warned me, I would have fallen into the fire. Thank you, child."

"It was not me," she said, trying to catch her breath. "It was Kateri. She told me to warn you."

"Kateri? Is she out of bed?"

"No. That's just it. She has been in bed all this time, as you know. But she said she saw you. That I must warn you."

Anastasia's eyes locked with the woman's. She ran back with her to Kateri's side.

They found her still wracked in pain with Smiling One weeping at her feet.

"What's wrong?" Anastasia shook her shoulder. "Why do you

cry?"

Smiling One wiped her face. "She told me to pray more often. She said I was to pray a rosary to Our Lady. That I was in danger of losing my faith. How did she know?"

Anastasia knelt beside Kateri's pallet and brushed the damp hair aside from her beaded forehead. "Go fetch Father Cholenec."

"No," said Kateri. "You go, Anastasia. I must talk with Marie Thérèse."

Anastasia did not protest. She rose and quickly left the longhouse.

"She is getting the priest to administer the last rites," Kateri said breathlessly. "But…" She gestured to the rags she wore. Part of her perpetual penance was to live like Christ; poor and chaste. She had not made herself new clothing as the years tolled on, but continued in her old clothes, clothes that became more ragged as the seasons changed. "I cannot receive my Lord like this. Do you have clothes I can borrow?"

Choked with emotion, Marie Thérèse could only nod. She ran to her pallet to retrieve a new skirt and top. She helped Kateri dress, cringing at each of her little cries of pain.

When at last she laid her down in her new clothes and brushed out her hair, the priest arrived. His eyes told her all, but instead of fear, she felt relief and joy. "Today, I will be in paradise," she told him.

The priest intoned the Latin words over her, anointing her with oil with the sign of the cross on her eyes, ears, mouth, heart, hands, and feet. For days, Kateri felt heavy with her pain, but as each portion of her was anointed, she felt the heaviness lift. When Anastasia elevated her shoulders to receive the Host, Kateri opened her mouth and felt the warmth of the Eucharist on her tongue. Slowly, it permeated throughout her body, radiating outward to her limbs. She felt her strength return, yet at the same time, knew it was not an earthly strength.

"Thank you, Father, she said, feeling the pain ease at last. "*Iesos kononronkwa.*"

Anastasia was holding Kateri's hand and felt the warmth in it leave. A tear escaped her eye and rolled down her cheek, but she could not help but feel happiness for the young woman before her who found her peace in God. She and Marie Thérèse sat at her side, humming the old Mohawk songs with Christian hymns. Anastasia closed her eyes and rocked with the ancient rhythms of a Mohawk chant, when Marie Thérèse gasped aloud.

"What is it?" she asked, a little weary of life herself.

"Look! Look at her face!"

Anastasia looked down.

Kateri's scars were gone, Instead, her skin smoothed to a waxy sheen and almost seemed to glow.

CHAPTER ELEVEN

They buried her at the riverbank beneath a cross. Yet even as the soil covered the coffin a trapper had made for her, more and more people arrived to pay their respects, both white and Iroquois. It was whispered along the river that the saint was dead and all seemed to know who was meant.

Smiling One kept watch day and night. She could not be convinced to leave. She was the most distraught of all.

Six days after she was buried and after many prayers were said, Father Cholenec readied for bed. He muttered his prayers and lifted himself from his knees. He climbed into bed and leaned over to blow out the candle when a light in the opposite side of the room startled him. The light seemed to grow, yet no candle burned there. He looked at the candle beside him and could discern no way the light could be reflected into that dark corner. He turned again toward the strange light and a figure began to form.

He leapt out of bed and clutched his crucifix. "What is it?" he said aloud...and the light answered.

There will be a fire.

"What? What is that?" He rubbed his eyes and felt his hands tremble.

There will be a fire. Take care. There will also be a brother here who dies a martyr's death. He is a martyr to the faith. Treat him accordingly.

The priest raised his hands to his mouth. "Mother of God. Kateri?"

Be mindful of what I said.

"Kateri!"

He stepped toward her but the light went out. Only the tiny flickering flame from his bedside candle lit the sparse room.

Father Cholenec fell to his knees, his mouth hanging open. What had he seen? What had he heard? "A vision," he croaked. He closed his eyes and began his evening prayers again.

More stories spread throughout the compound. Anastasia told of awakening and seeing Kateri at her bedside, beautiful and radiant. And even Father Fremin who had laughed at her request to become a nun, told in a shaken voice how he was visited by Kateri and told to paint her portrait so that she would inspire other Mohawks as she had been inspired by the prayer cards of the saints. Father Claude helped him.

Anastasia looked at Kateri's few possessions and held them to her chest. A blanket, a cup, a necklace of wampum shells. So few things. So great a life.

She felt a breath of air as the hide flap was pushed aside. Another had come to look at the place she had lived. She hugged those possessions tighter. "What do you want?" she asked as kindly as her broken heart allowed.

"May I have her blanket?" asked a man's voice.

Surprised, Anastasia rose. Garonhiague, the Christian chief of the Oneida, stood sorrowfully before her. "What would you—a great warrior chief—want with her poor blanket?"

"My wife is ill. It is said that those who pray and ask for Kateri's intercession are cured of their illnesses. But if my wife could touch her blanket I know she would be instantly cured."

"Why?" she asked, clutching the precious relics tighter. "Why do you want these things?"

"Don't you know? Kateri Tekakwitha was...*is*...a saint."

AUTHOR'S AFTERWORD

Instead of an ordinary biography, I chose to write Kateri's tale more like a novel, though the story itself is true. I have kept the main points true to her life while adding small details about the people she lived with, and creating what I believed were the motivations to certain events. We do not know, for instance, if Kateri experienced visions of the cross, but this theme was added to breathe life into her desire to do constant penance, to wear the cross, and live her life in chastity. Certainly something similar must have inspired her during her conversion process.

Most of the names of those Native Americans around her were unknown, but so that the narrative would flow I gave names to fictional people like Wild Flower and Sky Woman. Smiling One was a real person but I used a fictional name since her real name was lost to history.

Kateri was baptized on April 5, 1676, and unlike today when adults entering the Church receive the sacrament of Confirmation and first Holy Communion on the day they are baptized, usually at the Easter Vigil, Kateri did not receive her first Eucharist until Christmas Day in 1677. Kateri was known as a mystic, someone whose relationship with God is solitary and quiet, mostly spent in prayer and meditation. Kateri died at twenty-four years old, on April 17, 1680. Almost immediately a case was made for her canonization (the process by which the Church declares saints), but because the Church is cautious about whom it declares a saint, it wasn't until 1943 that the Church declared Kateri "Venerable," or worthy of veneration.

On June 22, 1980, Pope John Paul II beatified her in Rome, and on December 19, 2011, Pope Benedict XVI, approved the second miracle attributed to her and declared her a saint.

It should be noted that the Catholic Church does not "make saints." Rather, it is God who makes saints, but it is the Church that has always officially recognized their good works and close relationship to God by declaring them worthy of veneration. These are merely a special few of the millions who have gone unrecognized.

What makes a saint a saint? A relationship with God and the ability to spread that holiness to others. This makes them worthy to be emulated. Or, to put it another way, these are our spiritual heroes. In their lifetimes, they were able to convey this relationship by their lives of holiness. For some, they started out living ordinary lives, sometimes even as soldiers and disreputable people. Later, they came to know God and dedicated their lives to him in service to humanity in some way, by preaching, by writing about the spiritual life or interpretations of Scripture, or by going out in the world and doing for others.

Kateri Tekakwitha lived a simple life at a time and place where it was dangerous to be a Christian. She did not preach loudly nor did she build churches or schools, but by her simple living, her deep faith shown through her daily struggles, her love she showed for God, and her devotions to suffering in Jesus' name, she led the way for others to follow her example to come to God. Preaching need not be spoken aloud, nor do churches need to be built of wood and stone. Church is people, and for many Mohawks in her day, she was a beacon in the darkness, giving them a way of loving God they never dreamed of before.

Many people are more familiar with certain saints and less with others. For instance, almost everyone has heard of Saint Patrick and Saint Francis of Assisi. These, and many more, are saints who come from Europe. Though Christianity began in the Middle East in an unimportant country then known as Palestine and now known as Israel, Christianity is erroneously thought of as a mostly Western European religion, mostly because of Europe's adoption of Christianity as the state religion under the Holy Roman Emperor Constantine in the fourth century. But the Church has always recognized saints from all over the world, because people of faith exist in every corner of the world.

Why do we need saints from our own places on the planet? I'll give you an example. When I told a friend I was writing this story, she did not know who Kateri Tekakwitha was. When I told her she was a Mohawk saint my friend gasped in surprised. She put her hand on her heart and with great emotion said, "*I'm* Mohawk!" In her eyes, I saw the wisdom of declaring saints from all ethnic backgrounds and all walks of life. My friend would now have a special saint who understood *her* life. She had someone to talk to, pray with, and someone to emulate. That is why saints come in all shapes and sizes, and from all nations. And that is why God chose to come to earth, born as a man, so that our sorrows would be his sorrows, our pain his pain, our joy his joy.

The Sault Mission was eventually moved long after Kateri's death. Because she was so important a person in that region, her remains were moved to the new mission in Auriesville, New York.

Thanks for reading. You may contact me at authoracastell@gmail.com.

NOTES

There are a few words and terms worth explaining. I hope this will help clarify.

IROQUOIA   Now New York state

IROQUOIS   The term "Iroquois" is used to denote the five nations or five fires of the Iroquois Confederacy: Mohawk, Seneca, Oneida, Onondagas, And Cayuga. They were also known as the "Ho-den-na-sau-nee"—the People of the Longhouses.

"IESOS KONONRONKWA"   "Jesus, I love you."

LAKE OF THE SACRAMENT   Many of the missionary fathers named the places they discovered. This lake is now known as Lake George.

"SHE:KON, RIKEN:A"   When Father Boniface arrives, he calls this greeting, which means, "Greeting, little brothers!"

SHONKWAIA'TISHON   Literally, "He finished our bodies." This is a word used for Creator or God. Another is "Tharonhiawakon" or "He holds the heavens."

DISCUSSION GUIDE

1. In Kateri's time—and in some places in the world today—all people are not considered equal. How can one keep one's faith under those circumstances?

2. Why were some of the Mohawks so averse to Christianity?

3. Some saints did big things. Kateri did small things. Discuss the many ways one can serve God.

4. Kateri is often called the patron saint of ecology. Discuss why.

5. Why is it important to find saints you can relate to?

PARTIAL BIBLIOGRAPHY

The Venerable Servant of God, Kateri Tekakwitha. Positio of the Historical Section of the Sacred Congregation of Rites, Rome, English Edition, New York, 1940

Henri Béchard, S. J., *The Original Caughnawaga Indians*

Thomas Coffey, S. J., *Kateri Tekakwitha, America's Marvelous Maiden*, 1994

F.X Weiser, S. J., *Kateri Tekakwitha*

Sr. Mary Pelagia Litkowski, *Blessed Kateri Tekakwitha, Joyful Lover*, 1989

Evelyn M. Brown, *Kateri Tekakwitha: Mohawk Maiden*, Ignatius Press, 1958

Maureen McCauley, *Adventures with a Saint: Kateri Tekakwitha-Lily of the Mohawks*, 1992

Margaret R. Bunson, *Kateri Tekakwitha—Mystic of the Wilderness*, Our Sunday Visitor Publishing Division, 1992

Doug George-Kanentiio, *Iroquois Culture and Commentary*, Clear Light Publishers, Santa Fe, NM, 2000

Candy Moulton, *Everyday Life Among the American Indians*, Writer's Digest Books, Cincinnati, OH, 2001

Woodeene Koenig-Bricker, *365 Saints: Your Daily Guide to Wisdom and Wonder of Their Lives*, Harper San Francisco, 1995

NATIVE SPIRIT

CPSIA information can be obtained at www.ICGtesting.com
Printed in the USA
BVOW01s2204191214

380271BV00001B/19/P

9 781500 486624